A MURDER PLOT

The phone was picking up someone else's conversation. But the two voices were both so staticky it was hard for me to make them out. Just a few words here and there.

Harmless words, such as *kill.*

Murder.

Die.

These people sounded like killers! "Hector . . ." I was about to tell him what was going on. But then it hit me. What if the people talking on my line could hear me talking as well?

Panicking, I pressed the Channel button, trying to get rid of the voices. Instead the voices grew louder—and clearer.

An old man's voice: "It's all arranged, Beverly. Ms. Bates dies . . . tonight."

A young woman laughed happily. "What do I have to do?"

"Just be sure you're on board by seven. Pier Thirty-nine. Ms. Bates will be dead at midnight."

JOIN THE TEAM!

Do you watch GHOSTWRITER on PBS? Then you know that when you read and write to solve a mystery or unravel a puzzle, you're using the same smarts and skills the Ghostwriter Team uses.

We hope you'll join the team and read along to help solve the mysterious and puzzling goings-on in all of the GHOSTWRITER books!

Ghost writer®

DEADLINE

by **Eric Weiner**

illustrated by David Klein

A Children's Television Workshop Book

Bantam Books
New York Toronto London Sydney Auckland

DEADLINE
A Bantam Book/March 1996

Ghostwriter is a registered trademark of Children's Television Workshop.

Ghostwriter™ and ● ™
are trademarks of Children's Television Workshop.
All rights reserved. Used under authorization.

Written by Eric Weiner
Interior illustrations by David Klein
Cover design by Marietta Anastassatos
Cover photo of cruise ship: Pierre Kopp/WESTLIGHT

ISBN 0-553-48319-6
Published simultaneously in the United States and Canada

PRINTED IN THE UNITED STATES OF AMERICA

OPM   0 9 8 7 6 5 4 3 2 1

DEADLINE

It was a dark and stormy night.

It was a dark and stormy night.

It was a dark and stormy night.

Actually, it was a Sunday afternoon. I was sitting at my computer, typing the same line over and over.

I was in big trouble.

The next morning, Monday at nine sharp, our mystery stories were due in English class. Ms. Serling said this was what writers call a deadline. What it meant was, we had to hand in the stories tomorrow—or flunk. No excuses.

Our mysteries had to be at least twenty pages long, too. So far I had only one line.

I know what you're going to say. Believe me, I'd already

said it to myself about a zillion times. All day long I'd been mentally shouting at myself—

Yo, Lenni! You got the assignment three months ago. Why'd you wait till the day before it was due to start writing?

Well, for one thing, I didn't have an idea for my story. I didn't even have an idea for how to get an idea. I didn't even have an idea for how to get an idea for how to get an i—

Poof! Suddenly the computer screen went blank. Blue letters started typing—all by themselves. I sat up straight.

Two years ago our secret friend, Ghostwriter, started writing to our team. I guess I've almost gotten used to having a ghost write me messages. But it's not something you ever get *totally* used to, let me tell you.

Are you writing a story? Ghostwriter typed.

TRYING TO, I typed back. I HAVE TO WRITE A MYSTERY BUT I CAN'T GET STARTED.

The letters hung for a second while Ghostwriter thought. Then he wiped away my message and typed back, **Perhaps it would help if you say what your story is about, without worrying about grammar. Just spill out your ideas like water.**

That sounded good. Until I remembered . . .

THAT'S JUST IT, I typed. I DON'T HAVE AN IDEA! I STINK!

You don't stink, wrote Ghostwriter. **You're great.**

That helped a little. But I still sort of felt as if I stunk.

What about writing a mystery from your own life? Ghostwriter asked. **You could start with something that happened to you and then change it around to make it more mysterious.**

Yes! I smiled. Excellent plan.

But almost at once my smile turned back into a frown.

Ever since Ghostwriter started writing to me and my friends, he's been helping us solve real-life mysteries. With Ghostwriter's help we've been working to stop crimes here in Fort Greene, which is part of Brooklyn, New York, and in other places. But I couldn't write about any of those mysteries because Ghostwriter is a *secret*.

We figure there must be a very good reason why Ghostwriter writes only to us. Everyone on the team has pledged that we won't tell anyone about him.

I let out a moan, which came out sounding more like a scream, because just then the cordless phone started ringing and it startled me. I snatched up the phone.

"Hello?"

At first, nothing. Then a strange, deep voice said, "Hey."

"Hello?" I said again.

"Lenni." The voice sounded weird, mean. I shivered.

"Who's this?" I said.

The person said his name, but his voice was garbled and I couldn't make it out. I started to freak.

My dad's a jazz musician. He had a rehearsal that afternoon for a gig he was playing that night—a wedding in Queens. I was alone in our loft. Alone with some creepy caller who sounded hoarse, the way gangsters sound in movies.

And he knew my name.

Then the garbled voice said his name again.

And this time I figured out what he was saying: "It's Hector!"

Hector Carrero is nine. He's a member of our team.

"Hector, are you okay? You sound like Marlon Brando playing the Godfather. And why aren't you at the game?"

My friends and teammates were all at the Yankees game, watching the Yanks clobber Detroit.

Hector laughed, then coughed, then said, "Ow. Don't make me laugh. I woke up this morning with wicked laryngitis so my mom wouldn't let me go. She says they said on TV it's going to rain. So of course the sun is shining like crazy." More coughing. "It makes me so mad. I mean, it probably would have been better for me to be out in the sun, right?"

"Hector," I said, "don't talk so much. I can barely understand you and besides you're probably hurting your throat."

I guess he agreed with me because right away he got real quiet. "Listen, don't feel too bad," I told him. "I had to miss the game, too, and believe me, I feel worse than sick."

I explained about my deadline. I know it doesn't sound like much, being behind on your homework. But I'd trade that for laryngitis any day. When I put something off, I start getting this horrible squirmy feeling as if I swallowed a snake.

So why do I put things off all the time? That's a good question. I keep putting off figuring out the answer.

"Ghostwriter just wrote me about your story," Hector said in his whispery voice. "Said you might need some help."

Thank you, Ghostwriter!

"I've got nothing better to do," said Hector. "I could help you brainstorm if you like."

"Hector, did I ever tell you you're my favorite person in the whole world?"

He laughed, then said, "Ow!" again.

"Stop laughing," I told him.

"Stop being funny. Anyway, you need an idea for a murder mystery, right?"

"Need an idea? Not exactly. I would *kill* for an idea."

"Well . . . I've got one."

My mouth dropped open. "You do?"

"Check this out. These British people get these invitations to take a vacation on this tiny island. But when they get there, the island is deserted. And then . . ." He was already whispering, because of his throat, but now he lowered his voice even more, to sound creepy.

"One by one they start getting bumped off." He did some sound effects of people dying. "And what makes it really scary is . . . the guests know it has to be one of them who's doing the murders, but they don't know which one. . . ."

Even though I knew this was just a story, I started getting goose bumps. "Hector, this is so fabulous, I can't believe it," I gushed. "Just one thing. Why'd you say these people should be British? I mean, what do I know about British people?"

"Yeah, yeah," Hector agreed, "change that. Make some of the people Jewish like you and some of them Puerto Rican like me. 'Cause you know all about being you, right? And I can tell you anything you need to know about being from Puerto Rico." He coughed. "I figure you can write the first couple of chapters from what I just said, but after that I'll have to call you back as soon as I read more."

My excitement faded. "Read more? Hector, where's this from?"

"*And Then There Were None* by Agatha Christie. I started reading it last night and I couldn't put it down. I stayed up really late, which my mom says is why I got sick."

I sighed. "Hector, if this is an Agatha Christie book then I can't use it. That's plagiarism."

"Plaja who?"

"Stealing. I mean, that would be worse than just missing my deadline. Not only would I get an F, I'd probably get kicked out of school."

"Hey, that's where you're wrong," said Hector. "My English teacher says writers use old plots all the time. He says even Shakespeare did it. He took these old stories but told them in his own way and turned them into something new."

I sighed again. "Well, I'm no Shakespeare, believe me. I can get writer's block writing a shopping list."

Hector said something else, but this time his voice was so faint I couldn't make it out.

"What?" I asked.

"I didn't say anything," Hector said.

The faint voice kept talking in the background. And then—

Another faint voice answered the first voice.

The phone was picking up someone else's conversation. But the two voices were both so staticky it was hard for me to make them out. Just a few words here and there:

Dock . . . night . . . tonight . . . Laura . . .

"You don't hear that?" I asked Hector.

"Hear what?"

"There's someone else talking on our line."

"Cool. What are they saying?"

I listened hard:

Plan . . . Marnie . . . perfect . . . rich . . .

"Something about a plan," I said.

I pressed the receiver against my ear.

And then I heard a few other words . . .

Harmless words, such as *kill.*

Murder.

Die.

These people sounded like killers! "Hector—" I was about to tell him what was going on. But then it hit me. What if the people talking on my line could hear me talking as well?

Panicking, I pressed the Channel button, trying to get rid of the voices. Instead, the voices grew louder—and clearer.

An old man's voice: "It's all arranged, Beverly. Ms. Bates dies . . . tonight."

A young woman laughed happily. "What do I have to do?"

"Just be sure you're on board by seven. Pier Thirty-nine. Ms. Bates will be dead at midnight."

2

There was a tiny, awful click as the murderers hung up. I felt so shocked I didn't say a word.

"Are you still there or what?" Hector asked.

I nodded, which of course meant nothing to Hector since we were on the phone.

"Are you still listening to those people?" asked Hector. "Don't leave me out. What are they saying?"

"Hector . . . ," I began.

"Really? They're talking about me? How about that." Hector chuckled. Then sneezed. Then blew his nose really loudly.

"H-Hector," I stammered, "they're . . . they were planning a murder."

Hector paused. "No way." He laughed again. "That's just

like this old mystery movie I saw on TV last week. *Sorry, Wrong Number.* This woman is sick in bed. She's all alone and—"

"Hector! This was real! I just heard two people talking about killing someone. Tonight."

There was a stunned pause. Then Hector said, "C'mon, you really think they were serious?"

That was a good question. I had to think about that. But as I thought, the killers' conversation replayed in my mind. And not only had these people sounded serious, they'd sounded sure. Sure they could kill Ms. Bates and get away with it.

Along with being scared, I started getting mad.

"Hector, I swear to you, these people were serious."

"How do you know?"

Hector hadn't heard the killers talking, so I guess I couldn't expect him to be as worked up as I was. Still, it frustrated me that he didn't believe me.

Sometimes I don't get scared until after something scary happens. The killers were off the phone. Hector and I were alone again, and safe. But with every passing second, I was getting more frightened. I kept hearing that old man say, "Ms. Bates will be dead at midnight."

Dead at midnight.

Dead at midnight.

My chest started going in and out so fast I could barely talk. I gripped the phone as if it were a lifeline and I'd just fallen into the East River.

"You know what, Lenni?" Hector said. "If you really think they were serious—"

"I already told you!"

"Yeah, *sí, sí,* I know, I know. I'm thinking. You know

what? You'd better call the cops. And call a rally, too. I'll come over right away, okay?"

He hung up before I could say yes or thanks or anything. I hung up, too. But I didn't call the cops right away. What I did was, I looked around the loft, trying to calm down. There stood my electric keyboard, with a song I was working on clipped to the music stand. There on the old fridge was a note from Dad reminding me there was leftover Chinese food if I got hungry. Everything looked just the way it had one second ago—familiar and safe. It was hard to believe I'd heard what I'd just heard—

Two people plotting to take somebody's life.

There are a lot of bad things in the world. People polluting the environment. People stealing and doing drugs. But taking somebody's life? I can't imagine anything worse than that happening in the whole entire universe.

"Officer Franklin Dixon," said a gruff male voice when I punched in the numbers for the police station.

"Lieutenant McQuade, please."

"Lieutenant McQuade is off for the weekend. How can I help you?"

Lieutenant McQuade has worked with us on lots of our crime-solving adventures. He's getting to be a pretty good friend to our team. He knows us, and he trusts us. "I'd really like to speak to Lieutenant McQuade if I could."

"Well, like I said, you can't. Sorry. Now how can I—"

"Do you have his home phone number?"

"Yeah, I do. But what's this about?"

"Well, I just heard these two people planning a murder."

That got his attention. "What do you mean? Where?"

"On the phone. They were on my channel on the cordless. Killers. Two of 'em."

"Uh-huh. And they said what, exactly?" He was back to sounding bored again.

"They said they were going to kill somebody. Ms. Bates. And then something about meeting at Pier Thirty-nine by seven. I guess that's where they're going to kill her. Or, you know what? I just realized something. He said to be on board by seven. There's probably a boat at that pier. They're going to take Ms. Bates on this boat and—"

"Let's just stick to what you actually heard, okay?"

"That's all I heard. Then they hung up."

I waited. So did Officer Dixon.

"What's the matter?" I asked. "Don't you believe me?" When I get upset, my voice gets really high. Which is bad, because it makes me sound even younger than I am, which is only twelve.

"Calm down, calm down," said the policeman. "Of course I believe you. It's just that if that's all you heard, it's not a lot for us to go on, you understand?"

"What do you mean?"

"Well, which Pier Thirty-nine are we talking about here? There are a lot of piers in Brooklyn, you know. And then there's Jersey. And how about Manhattan? It's an island. Loads of piers."

"I guess you'll just have to send cops to every Pier Thirty-nine in the area," I said.

"Yeah. Kid, I don't want to be blunt. But the thing is, people say things all the time, you know what I mean? 'I'm going to kill So-and-so.' 'I wish So-and-so were dead.' You've probably said that kind of thing yourself. 'I'm so mad at my brother I could murder him.' Am I right?"

"I don't have a brother."

"Look, the point is, we have a hard enough time catching

all the people who really do commit crimes. We don't have time to worry about people who just talk about it."

"But—"

"I took down what you said," interrupted Officer Dixon. "Lenni Frazier. Heard people on phone planning a murder. I'll leave a note on Lieutenant McQuade's desk for tomorrow, Monday. How's that?"

"Monday! Didn't you hear what I said? They're going to kill her tonight!"

"Ms. Frazier, I've got the information. Now if you don't mind, I'm very busy and—"

My father would have had about six and a half fits if he'd seen what I did next. I hung up on Officer Dixon. I hung up on a man who was not only a grown-up but a police officer!

Dad says sometimes I let my temper get the better of me. He also says I don't always have the proper respect for adults. But on the other hand, if you ask me, adults don't always have the proper respect for kids. I'm sure Officer Dixon would have taken me a whole lot more seriously if I'd sounded twenty instead of twelve.

It just made me so mad. The way he was so casual about the whole thing.

As casual as the killers.

I stared at the phone. On our team I'm known for being blunt and sort of tough. I guess people would be surprised if they knew how scared I get on the inside. Like right now. I was shaking. I expected Officer Dixon to call back and yell at me. Or burst through the door and arrest me for being rude. But the phone stayed silent and the front door stayed locked. *Officer Dixon doesn't know me from a hole in the wall*, I told myself.

And he doesn't care, either.

Maybe that's why I started getting this terrible cold feeling of being all alone.

Then I remembered Hector's second suggestion. Call a rally.

I don't know if you've ever been on a team, but it always takes me by surprise—in a really good way—when I remember I have this band of friends. Friends who'll stick by me whenever things get bad. I ran over to the sofa and yanked out a notebook from under a pile of schoolbooks, which all spilled onto the floor. I flipped to a clean page and pulled off the pen I always wear around my neck for emergencies like this.

"RALLY—L," I wrote in big block letters.

Instantly a swirl of green sparkles flew around the letters, lifting them into the air. I watched as Ghostwriter zoomed the message out the window.

I kept watching, waiting for the return message to fly back from the team.

It didn't come.

Okay, I told myself, trying to stay calm. *I know what's happening. The baseball game is so exciting, they probably all missed the rally message. No big deal.*

But as I sat there with my blank notebook in my lap, my legs started to tremble. I was getting a terrible case of the creeps.

Hector hadn't come yet. Dad was at rehearsal. The team didn't answer.

I was all alone.

Alone with horrible news.

Ms. Bates, whoever she was, was about to die.

3

I couldn't sit still. I paced. Then I called Hector back, but there was no answer. He'd already left.

Our loft is right above the Fernandez bodega and the apartment where my teammates Gaby and Alex Fernandez live. If Dad has to leave me alone, he always makes sure that Mr. or Mrs. Fernandez is downstairs in case I need them. I never need them but it's nice knowing they're there.

Well, now I needed them.

I looked at the clock for the umpteenth time. 4:21. About fifteen minutes had gone by since I'd heard the killers on the phone. I ran to open the door and fiddled with the locks. Then I flung open the door and—

A figure lunged out of the dark, his fist raised to pound me in the face. I screamed. So did—

Hector.

He'd just run up the steps and was about to knock.

We both staggered around the room a little, trying to catch our breath. "What's the matter with you?" he gasped in his hoarse sore-throat voice. "I rush over here and then you wait at the door and scream in my face?"

"Sorry, sorry."

I must have looked pretty pale because he grabbed my arm and said, "It's okay, it's okay, *mi amiga.*" He flashed that big grin of his.

Hector is short and slight with dark hair and big, dark eyes like buttons. Right now, though, his eyes were narrow. "You've been eating peanuts recently, haven't you?" he whispered.

Hector is into reading mysteries in a big way. He'll take two or three out of the library and read them all in a week. He's also into acting like whatever detective he reads about. Sometimes he calls himself Sherlock Carrero, or Hector Poirot (after the detective in Agatha Christie's books). Fact is, he's a very good detective.

"How'd you know?" I asked, worried. "Is my breath bad?"

Hector laughed and pointed. "You've got little bits of shell stuck in your hair. And what's this? Wow. Beautiful!"

He was touching one of my earrings. They're emerald pendants, green and shiny jewels. I knew why he was so surprised. I usually hate wearing makeup or lipstick or anything like that. I only wear the earrings when I'm inside the loft. That's partly because I don't want to risk losing them, and partly because I don't want anyone to see them on me.

"They were my mom's," I explained, blushing as I pulled my head away.

There was more I could have told him. Like the reason

I'd been wearing Mom's earrings this week. Mom's birthday was coming up in two weeks. Or what would have been her birthday. She died of cancer when I was seven. Her birthday is always a hard time of year for me. It makes me miss her so much.

But the instant these feelings come up in me, I get mad and try to shut them down. Hector must have seen the look on my face, because all he said was, "They must be worth a fortune." It was his way of changing the subject, in case I didn't want to talk about it, which I didn't.

"Let's get to work," I said.

"Right. What did the team say?" Hector asked.

I held up the blank notebook.

"They're too busy watching baseball, I guess," said Hector. He coughed and wheezed.

"That's what I figured. You sound horrible, by the way."

Horrible was putting it mildly. Hector sounded as if he'd swallowed a ninety-year-old man. He looked washed out, too. I felt bad that I had dragged him out of bed. What if Officer Dixon was right? What if the people on the phone weren't serious? "You want chicken soup? I can stick some instant in the microwave."

"Great," Hector said, hunting for the Kleenex box. He blew his nose, then gave me his best grin, only it looked a little weaker than usual. While I made the soup, I told him what the police officer had said.

"Then it's up to us," said Hector. His voice scratched badly, as if each word tore his throat.

"Maybe you shouldn't talk," I suggested, handing him a steaming mug. "Just write."

He nodded, took a sip of soup, smiled to show he liked it, then wrote in my notebook, "Delic—"

I guessed the word before he wrote any more. "Delicious," I said. Underneath that I wrote, "Thanks."

Hector rolled his eyes. "You don't have to write," he croaked. "I can still hear!"

"Sorry." I giggled.

Just then green sparkles swirled around our notes. We both smiled. Our secret friend was joining the conversation. So it was a good idea for me to write after all. This way Ghostwriter could listen in. I was feeling less and less alone.

"Ghostwriter, we need to warn somebody named Ms. Bates," Hector wrote. He sucked thoughtfully on the cap of his pen. Then he wrote, "We don't have much info."

That's just what the cop had said. Not much info.

Sometimes, when our team is at the very beginning of a mystery and we don't have many clues yet, I have trouble believing that we'll ever solve it. This case was worse than most. I had heard two voices. They'd come out of the static of a phone conversation and then—they were gone. How could we ever hope to find them again?

"Tell Ghostwriter what's going on," I said to Hector. "Maybe he'll have an idea."

I watched while Hector scribbled an update. Ghostwriter spun some of Hector's letters into a reply. That is terrifying! We must find Ms. Bates at once!

I agreed with Ghostwriter, but it didn't help much.

Hector made a sound to get my attention, then walked his fingers across the page of the notebook as if they were legs. Just like in the TV ad for the yellow pages.

"Let your fingers do the walking!" I cried. "Right! Why didn't I think of that!"

I started running around the loft, searching for the phone book white pages. I found them under Dad's ukulele case.

(Dad can play almost anything and there are instruments all over our loft, on the walls, on the floor, everywhere.) I flipped to the Bs. Hector watched me. I groaned.

"This is hopeless," I said.

Hector shook his head to show me that I was wrong, that it wasn't hopeless. That's another good thing about being on a team. At any moment, there's bound to be at least one kid who's feeling confident, and he can bring up the rest.

"But look, Hector," I said, "there are about fifty Bateses in Brooklyn." I groaned again. "Hector? Do you think my cordless could pick up a call from Manhattan?"

He shrugged.

"Great," I said. "Then we don't know for sure that Ms. Bates lives in Brooklyn. There are probably a hundred Bateses living in Manhattan. And then there's Queens, the Bronx, and—"

I stopped short. "What am I whining about? Someone's life is at stake," I said. "We'll just have to call them all." I wrote the comment down for Ghostwriter.

Hector shook his head, crossed out what I'd written. "What would we say?" he croaked. " 'Hi, can you tell us if you're going to be murdered tonight?' Besides, it'll take too long."

I glanced at the clock. Hector was right. It was already close to five.

Ghostwriter took all the letters on the page and squinched them together into one long, thin message: We've got to narrow down the list!

"That's exactly what I was thinking," I said.

The letters stretched back to their normal size, then spun again. Please write down everything you re-member from this phone conversation, wrote

Ghostwriter. **Perhaps I can help if I have more information.**

"Sure," I said aloud, which Ghostwriter couldn't hear, but then I started saying everything I could remember and Hector wrote it down. As it turned out, that helped me remember more details.

I began by telling Ghostwriter all the stray words I'd heard when the phone line was staticky:

Dock, night, boat, tonight, Laura, plan, the idea, Marnie, perfect, blood, rich, kill, murder, die.

Then I had Hector write down the things I'd heard the killers say really clearly, which I've already told you about. About killing Ms. Bates.

Ghostwriter zipped through the message. Then he circled two names, *Laura* and *Marnie.* Then he took all the words and twisted them into a big question mark.

"Maybe those are the killers' names," I said, writing.

"But U said 1 killer = old man," Hector wrote back.

It took me a moment to decipher what Hector had written. He was leaving out words to save writing time. When I figured out what Hector meant, though, I realized he was right. One of the killers on the phone was an old man. So Laura and Marnie couldn't be the two killers. I was stumped.

What if there are more than two killers? wrote Ghostwriter.

That was possible. But it didn't help us solve the mystery.

"Wait a minute!" Hector gasped. He was so excited he spoke instead of writing. "What if . . ."

He kept talking, but his voice was so hoarse I couldn't understand him. I shook my head. He started writing furiously. I leaned over his shoulder, reading out the words as he wrote them. "What. If. Marnie. Is. Ms. Bates's. First . . ."

"Name!" I said, catching on at last. I grabbed the phone book, which I had stupidly closed, so I had to find the B section all over again. Then I looked up Marnie Bates.

The phone book showed no Marnie Bates.

Then I tried for Laura, running my finger quickly down the L part of the Bates list:

BATES, L 16 MANNING ST. **555-8938**

BATES, L A 449 W 23 ST. **555-5804**

BATES, L C 1025 WALKER ST. **555-3241**

BATES, L M 313 HITCHCOCK ST. **555-4483**

BATES, L P 505 MILL AV. **555-2318**

BATES, LEONARD 981 2ND AV. **555-8554**

I grimaced. No Laura either.

I shook my head, feeling very disappointed. Our mystery had come to an end. Ms. Bates would die, or not die. We'd never know. There was nothing we could do.

But Hector peered at the phone book and jabbed his finger at the page. He grunted. I looked where he was pointing—

BATES, L M 313 HITCHCOCK ST. **555-4483**

"Laura Marnie," I gasped as Ghostwriter made the letters *L* and *M* jump up and down with excitement. I ran to the phone. Then I ran back to the phone book, because I'd already forgotten the number. I punched it into the keypad.

The woman who answered had this soft voice that I liked instantly. "Hi, this is Laura Bates," she said.

I felt as if I'd just gotten the President on the line. "Oh, wow. I am so glad I found you I can't tell you. Listen, this is going to sound really strange but—"

Ms. Bates let out a bloodcurdling scream.

Stunned, I dropped the phone on the floor.

I snatched it up, but—*whoops!*—I hit the Disconnect button.

I redialed, punching the numbers as fast as I could. Too fast. I had to try a couple of times. Hector was saying something, but I couldn't understand what. He wrote frantically and held up the notebook. "HIT REDIAL!" read his message.

I'd just finished dialing. A little boy answered, "Hello?"

"Is this . . . Laura Bates?" I gasped. Which was stupid. Obviously it wasn't Laura, but I wasn't thinking too clearly.

"Laura who?" asked the boy.

"Sorry, wrong number," I told him. Then I pressed Flash

to disconnect. "I'm so stupid," I told Hector. "You're right. I just have to press Redial."

For some reason Hector shook his head violently and waved his arms again. I listened to the little tune of beeps as the phone placed the call.

"Hello?" said the same young boy. That's when I realized what Hector was trying to tell me. Redial calls the very last number you dialed. "Sorry," I said, and hung up again.

All this time, I could hear Ms. Bates's horrible scream ringing in my ears. I pictured her lying on the floor of her apartment with a knife in her back. With every passing second, her life was draining away!

Finally I got the number right.

"Hi, this is Laura Bates," the woman's voice answered just as before.

My jaw dropped. I stared at the phone in amazement.

"Oh," I said, "that's a relief! You're—"

Then she screamed just like last time.

Then she beeped.

It was her answering machine! What a crazy message!

The answering machine kept beeping. And when it finally stopped beeping, the machine shut off without pausing to give me a chance to record my message.

"Tape full," wrote Hector after I told him what happened.

"Great," I said. I flopped down on the sofa next to Hector. One hour of detective work, and already I felt exhausted. "This Laura must be a wild person," I said. I was remembering her scream on the machine.

Hector nodded. He looked worried. He wrote for a moment, then handed me the notebook. "Wild person = some 1 who might get in trouble real EZ."

I sat up again. "Yeah, you're right." I handed back the notebook. "So what do we do now?"

Hector shrugged, then wrote, "Call till L.M. answer."

"Keep calling till Laura answers?" I deciphered. I made a face. "I don't like it. What if she's sleeping and then she wakes up and goes out without playing her messages?" I thought for a second. "Hey," I said. "Now we know where she lives."

"& Hitchcock St. is close," wrote Hector.

Hector and I stared at each other. I knew what he was thinking, because I was thinking the same thing. Up until now we'd been working in the safety of the loft. If we walked out of here, the game would change. Somewhere outside lurked two cold-blooded killers. We might be headed right for their lair.

"You think we should wait for the team?" I asked.

Hector didn't answer. Hector's not what I'd call a cautious kid. Once there was a bomb threat in his school. He raced back into the building because he remembered that our teammate Casey was sneaking a nap in the school library. So when I saw Hector hesitating now, it scared me.

"Look," I said. "We know the killers are meeting on board some ship at seven. How dangerous could it be to go over to Ms. Bates's apartment now?" I was trying to convince myself as much as I was trying to convince Hector.

Hector shut the notebook with a bang and stood up. He headed for the door.

I felt a pang of fear—there was no turning back now. "Hold it," I said. I grabbed my purple backpack and slung it over one shoulder as I ran to the fridge. I scribbled a note for Dad just in case he came home before I did. I was in such a rush that I didn't get stuck on what to say. The words poured out just the way Ghostwriter said—like water. I used the saxophone magnet to stick my note on the fridge door next to Dad's note to me.

Outside, the air was warm and breezy. Not a cloud in the sky. Cars, taxis, and buses honked angrily. Pedestrians strolled. Shoppers squeezed the fruit outside the Fernandez bodega and the Korean grocery store on the corner. Life as usual in Fort Greene. Again I had trouble believing that somewhere in the middle of all this two people were plotting a murder.

The building at 313 Hitchcock Street turned out to be a small brownstone with one broken window and a sign that said APARTMENT TO RENT. The sign looked old. Fort Greene isn't a very rich part of town. Just the opposite. Still, even here apartments are scarce. If this was Laura's home, I figured she didn't have much more money than Dad and me.

Hector and I stood outside, looking up at the building, as if it might be haunted.

"C'mon," I said.

We hurried up the steps and through the front door. Most of the mailboxes in the entrance area didn't have names on them. Some had been pried open like sardine cans. But we could see Laura's box. 1A.

The smell of fresh paint hit me hard. The building's inner door was propped open with an old paint-spattered bucket. A white dropcloth covered the dingy hallway floor. From inside the building we heard laughter. We followed the smell of the paint and the sound of the voices back to Apartment 1A.

This door was also open. We walked toward it slowly.

Then Hector reached out to knock on the door frame.

"Freeze!" barked a loud, gruff voice.

We peered into the apartment. Standing on a ladder and pointing a wet roller at us like a rifle was a tall young man with bristly, dark hair. His hair was speckled with white, but that was just paint. He was wearing white overalls that said FRANK AND JOE across the front in block letters. He was in the middle of painting the ceiling.

"I just painted that door frame," he told us. "You mess it up, you can repaint it yourselves."

"Sorry," I said. "Um, is this Laura Bates's apartment?"

"You got it."

It wasn't the man on the ladder who answered me. It was a second man, who was also wearing Frank-and-Joe overalls.

He was working on the wall at the other end of the room with another roller.

This second painter was tall and thin like his partner, but he had long, blond hair in a ponytail. Unlike his partner, he was soft-spoken and gentle-sounding. I immediately started asking him all my questions.

"Is she home?"

"Does it look like she's home?" answered the painter with dark hair. I was really starting to dislike him.

"Well, do you know where she is or when she'll be back?"

Hector asked that, and even I could barely understand him. I translated. I also introduced myself and Hector. The nice painter with the ponytail said his name was Joe. He said his partner's name was Frank. I could have guessed that. "But we don't know where Laura is," Joe added. "Sorry."

They kept working. Hector and I looked at each other. A silent question flew back and forth between us: *Can we trust these painters? Maybe they're working for the killers!*

On the other hand, we needed help finding Laura.

"Uh . . . ," I said. "We really need to find her, 'cause, uh . . . we think she might be in trouble."

Joe stopped painting again. He looked concerned. "What kind of trouble?"

"Well, uh, the worst kind." I paused. There wasn't any good way to say this. "Someone is planning to murder her."

There was a silence; then Frank started laughing. "Oooo," he said, as if he was really scared. Then he sang the music from *The Twilight Zone*, "Deedle-deedle, deedle-deedle . . ."

"You're friends of Laura's?" Joe asked kindly.

"No, we never met her," I admitted.

"Oh." He seemed confused. "Then how—"

"We heard two people talking on the phone about killing Ms. Bates."

"Ah." Joe smiled. "Like *Sorry, Wrong Number,* eh?"

Hector and I exchanged glances.

"This isn't a joke," I said.

"You really heard voices on the phone?" Frank asked.

"Yes!"

Frank whistled. "Far out. But you have the wrong Bates."

"But they said Laura," I insisted.

"And Marnie," Hector added, though I was probably the only one who understood him.

"Then you have the wrong Laura Bates," Frank added, rolling his roller in the paint tray.

"Look, the Laura who lives here is probably the world's sweetest person," Joe explained. "Everyone loves this Laura. She has zero enemies. None."

"She also doesn't have a dime," said Frank.

"The point is," said Joe, "what's the motive? Why would anyone want to hurt her?"

Joe was right. Whoever was planning to kill Laura would need a very good reason.

"I don't know what the motive is," I admitted. It felt like when the teacher calls on you and you have to say you haven't done your homework. That situation was going to happen to me in school the next day.

"You know what I think the trouble is?" asked Joe, his eyes twinkling. "I think the two of you have caught the same disease we have. Laura's got it too. Mystery-itis."

"Mystery-itis?" I asked.

Joe gestured with his roller at a tall bookcase completely covered with dropcloths. "Take a look behind there."

We walked into the room, stepping carefully around the

trays and buckets of paint. Hector pulled back one of the cloths. He moaned—with pleasure, but it almost sounded like pain.

From top to bottom the shelves were lined with mysteries—mystery novels, mystery plays, mystery screenplays. Books with titles such as *Deathtrap, Sleuth,* and *Corpse!* There were complete collections of Sherlock Holmes, Dashiell Hammett, Raymond Chandler, and Agatha Christie. Laura owned children's mysteries as well—the complete Nancy Drew and Hardy Boys, all in a row.

Hector wrote me a note. "Want meet Laura!"

I nodded. I was thinking about Laura's strange answering machine message. That bloodcurdling scream. It made sense to me now. Mystery-itis!

I glanced around the rest of the studio apartment. Almost all of Laura's stuff was hidden under lumpy white dropcloths.

"Oh, wow," I said.

Leaning against the wall by the door was an oil painting. It was a portrait of a tall, beautiful redheaded woman. The woman's eyes stared right at me. It was as if there were someone else in the apartment with us.

"Laura," I said softly.

"Two points," said Frank.

"She's . . . beautiful," I said.

Neither painter answered me, but I could tell they both agreed. You'll probably think I'm exaggerating. But I could tell a lot about Laura just from the painting. I could tell she was wise, funny, kind, and somehow sad. What I was thinking was, *Joe is right. Why would anyone want to hurt this woman?*

Frank said, "There's actually a typical Laura story behind that painting. She spent three months typing for the artist who painted it. He kept promising he would pay her next week, next week. He couldn't afford to pay her a single penny. So he gave her that painting instead."

"She's way too trusting," agreed Joe sadly, and Frank nodded.

"How do you two know Laura?" I asked. It wasn't any of my business. But I wanted to make sure they weren't lying—and in on the murder plot.

"We're all mystery writers," Joe said.

"Trying to be," Frank corrected. "None of us has published a word. In the meantime, Laura is a typist and we're house painters, as you can see."

"We're all in the same mystery-writing class," Joe added. "With Ed Poe."

Hector made a squawking sound.

"You know Ed Poe?" asked Frank. "You really know your mysteries, huh, kid?"

"Who's Ed Poe?" I asked, feeling left out.

"Ed Poe wrote a couple of best-selling mysteries twenty years ago," said Joe. He wiped some paint from his face with the back of his hand. "Really great books. Then he got writer's block. Hasn't published a new book since seventy-six. He says he hasn't had a single new story idea in twenty years."

I could sympathize with that. Twenty years from now I'd probably just be finishing my mystery assignment for school.

"He's a great teacher, though," Joe added.

They kept talking about Poe, but I wasn't listening anymore. And from the look on Hector's face, I could see that he wasn't listening, either. We were both staring at Laura's painting, practically hypnotized. Her hair blazed like flaming copper. She had the thinnest, prettiest nose I'd ever seen. Like an exclamation point down the middle of her face.

"This like TV mystery," wrote Hector. "Old b&w movie *Laura*. Detective falls in love with woman after she's murdered, just by looking at portrait."

Falls in love, eh? Normally I would have teased Hector about that. But at the moment I was liking Laura too much to tease anyone. I know it's crazy, having such a big reaction to a painting. But it happened, what can I say?

I took Hector's notebook and wrote "I PROMISE" in bold letters. Underneath that I wrote a pledge. This wasn't going to be like that movie Hector saw. We were going to save Laura and get to know her before she was murdered, not after!

Hector nodded and signed his name under mine. Ghost-writer signed, too.

I glanced at my watch. 6:03. Time was running out, but I didn't feel panicked. We were in Laura's apartment, after all. We had almost found her.

"Now if you kids don't mind," Frank said, moving his ladder past us, "we need to work."

"We're not leaving until Laura comes back," I said firmly.

"Oh yes you are," Frank said, even more firmly.

"We have to warn her," I said.

"Leave her a note," Frank suggested.

"No. We need to warn her in person."

"I'm afraid," said Joe, "that you'll have a very long wait. She's not coming back tonight. Because of the paint fumes."

Great. Any confidence I was feeling drained away fast. Laura would go to Pier 39, wherever that was, before we got a chance to speak to her. And that meant . . .

Laura was going to die. There was nothing I could do.

Joe had finished the far wall. He rolled a large piece of furniture back into place. Then he pulled off the dropcloth with a flourish, like a magician doing a trick.

I gasped when I saw what was underneath.

Underneath the cloth stood Laura's old-fashioned rolltop desk. And on the desk, next to her cruddy old Smith-Corona electric typewriter, lay Laura's little black appointment book. Normally I wouldn't consider snooping in someone's personal stuff. I felt very funny about it. But Laura's life was on the line. I crossed the room. Hector followed.

"What do you think you're doing?" demanded Frank.

"Please," I said. "I know you don't believe us. Nobody believes us. But I get the feeling you like Laura and—"

Frank blushed.

"And, well, so do I, even though I've never even met her. And—" I was getting this lump in my throat, as if Laura had been my closest friend. The lump made it a little hard to talk.

Hector and I made some detectives. Him with laryngitis, me with a lump.

"And we've got to try to find her so we can warn her and—"

"Oh, go ahead and look," Frank said.

"Thank you."

I flipped through the appointment book until I came to the page for that day. My heart sank. The page was blank. No entry. Now what?

Hector rolled a blank sheet of paper into the typewriter. He flicked on the power and typed with two fingers: "Maybe she keeps a diary and she wrote the info in there."

Ghostwriter's green glow read Hector's message. Only members of our team can see Ghostwriter, but I stood between the painters and the typewriter, just to be safe.

I looked at the desk. It had all these different little cubbyholes. Stamps, envelopes, rubber bands, paper clips, and other stationery stuff were stored inside. No diary. But nestled in the bottom cubbyhole I spotted a small black piece of paper. I pulled it out.

It was an invitation. CAPTAIN BLOOD'S ANNUAL BOAT PARTY, it said in gloppy red letters.

Captain Blood? I didn't like the sound of that. Drops of blood were drawn around Blood's name.

MUSIC. DANCING. DINNER. MAGIC BY PRESTO. AND—

The next word was mostly blanks, along with a stick figure hanging from a noose like in a game of Hangman. The word was:

__ __ R __ __ __

Down at the bottom of the invitation were more instructions:

BE ON BOARD NO LATER THAN 7:00. THE BOAT LEAVES FROM—

The next two words pricked my skin like needles.

PIER 39.

Oh, wow, I thought as I watched Ghostwriter read the invitation. A boat party. Laura was invited. Someone was going to kill her at the party!

The invitation included directions. I flicked my wrist and looked at my watch, but my heart was racing so hard that at first I couldn't even tell the time.

6:11.

We had to move fast.

Just then the typewriter started typing—by itself. I quickly put my fingers on the keyboard to make it seem as if I were the one typing.

I think you should inform the police, typed Ghostwriter.

I WILL, I typed back, BUT I BET THEY WON'T LISTEN.

Under no circumstances should you go to this boat party alone!!!! Ghostwriter typed so fast the keys stuck together.

WE DON'T HAVE A CHOICE, I typed back. As I typed those words, I realized they were true. I was going to see this through—no matter what.

The typewriter engine whined and hummed for a moment. Then Ghostwriter typed, I'll tell the team to meet you there.

GREAT, I typed. I turned off the machine. I pulled my backpack off one shoulder so I could stuff the invitation into the front pocket. I nodded to Hector. We started toward the door. "Well," I told the painters, my voice shaking, "thanks."

"You're going?" Joe asked, sounding surprised. "I thought you wanted to warn Laura."

"If she comes back, please tell her what we said."

I backed out the door. Then we hurried down the hall without looking back.

We kept hurrying until we were out of sight of the building and halfway down the block. Hector made me call the cops again. They didn't sound any more interested in the case than last time.

Outside, the air had turned chilly. Dark clouds dotted the sky. I started to run, but Hector put a hand on my arm, slowing me down.

"We don't have time," I barked, trying to pull my arm free. "We're going to miss her!"

He held up his notebook. The letters spun crazily, like water gurgling down a drain. Then Ghostwriter got them all in the right position. It was a note from the team:

We got your message. Ghostwriter wrote to us on the Yankee Stadium scoreboard! We'll meet you at the pier.

"Yes!" I said. "C'mon!"

We sprinted down the block toward the entrance to the subway. Ghostwriter raced above our heads, reading all the street signs we passed.

Talk about a deadline.

We had to keep Laura from getting on that ship.

"We're going to miss the boat," I said, pacing up and down the subway car. "We're going to miss it, we're going to miss it, we're going to miss it!"

Hector held up his notebook. He'd written, "We won't miss it."

"We willllll," I moaned.

The underground train was moving more slowly than ketchup out of a bottle. Then the train stopped altogether, the metal wheels grinding against the tracks.

"C'mon!" I said, as if the train could hear me. "C'mon!"

There was only one other passenger in our car. He was a big, burly bear of a man in a greasy gray three-piece suit. The suit made him look like a businessman. But he had a long shock of Day-Glo orange hair down the middle of his head. It was an orange Mohawk.

The orange-haired man kept checking his watch, shifting nervously from foot to foot, getting up, sitting down, getting up, muttering, studying the wall map. I guess we weren't the only ones in a big rush.

"This is so horrible," I wailed. "We finally figure out where Pier Thirty-nine is, and then the stupid train doesn't move— C'mon!" I raised my voice almost to a shout. Believe it or not, the train started again the minute those words left my mouth.

Then I saw the expression on Hector's face. He was looking behind me. I turned.

The big man with the orange Mohawk loomed over me. He had big, crumpled features that made him look like a human bulldog. He smiled an oily smile.

Mom once wrote a fairy tale in which people in a kingdom wear their souls on the outside, right on their sleeves where everybody can see them. Nevertheless, their princess still judges people wrong, because she doesn't bother to look at their souls. Mom wrote the story for me. It's because I have this habit of deciding what I think of someone about one second after I meet them. Mom was always trying to get me to be more patient.

I still haven't learned that lesson. One look at this guy

with the strange hair and I knew he was mean and bad and up to no good. I was very unhappy that Hector and I were trapped on the same subway car with him.

"Pier Thirty-nine?" he asked. "You said Pier Thirty-nine, didn't you? Soooo, you're going to Captain Blood's boat party, are you?" He chuckled. "Correct me if I'm wrong. Go ahead, feel free to correct me. Can't correct me, am I correct?"

He was talking a mile a minute. He put a forefinger on my Red Hot Chili Peppers T-shirt and said, "Whoops. A spot."

When I looked down he ran his finger right up to my nose and laughed. "Oldest trick in the book," he said. "You must feel pretty dumb for falling for it."

Actually what I felt was that temper of mine starting to rise. The man stuck out a big hand. "My name's—"

He threw back his head and roared like a lion: *"Presto! The Magnificent!"*

I was so stunned it took me a moment to place the name.

"Wait a minute. Presto the magician?"

"Correct again. Whoops"—he pointed—"another spot."

I'm ashamed to admit it, but I fell for the same trick twice. Presto roared with laughter.

I was feeling a lot better. "Hector," I said, "it's Presto. The entertainment for tonight's party." As if Hector couldn't hear Presto shouting. But what I meant was, we were safe. We were with the magician. The boat couldn't possibly leave without us now.

Or so I thought. But right then Presto checked his watch and started grumbling, "The boat's going to leave without me! Oh, man—then I won't get paid. What time have you got?" he growled, pulling Hector's wrist toward him.

Presto bent over so that his big head was right up against Hector's watch.

Except that Hector's watch was gone.

Hector wheezed in amazement. Presto laughed. Then he held up Hector's black Swatch, dangling it back and forth. "Fooled ya," he said. "The hand is quicker than the eye."

Presto gave back the watch and patted Hector's shoulder. "What's the matter with you, son? Can't speak? Someone steal your voice? Well, you can't blame that on me, I'm a great magician but I'm not that good! Ha ha!"

"He has laryngitis," I said. As if to show the magician what I was talking about, Hector sneezed and coughed.

Presto rolled his eyes and backed away, big hands in the air. "What are you trying to do, get me sick?" He produced a blue-and-yellow handkerchief and coughed into it. Instantly it changed into a green-and-red handkerchief. Then it disappeared altogether. Hector clapped.

"Not bad," I said grudgingly.

"Not bad? You call that a compliment, twerp? I'm—"

Back went the head for another roar: *Presto, the Magnificent!*

Hector held up his notebook. "How did you do that?"

"I told you. The hand is quicker than the eye. Which is why my party invitation is now in"—he turned to me—"your backpack."

"No way."

But when I opened the front pocket of my pack there were two invitations inside. Just like mine, there was that hangman game on the center of Presto's invitation:

— — — — —R

"How'd you do that?" I said. Now he had me asking.

Presto grinned like a shark. He was also sweating. "You're impressed, huh?"

I hated to admit it, but like the princess in my mother's fairy tale, I might have judged this guy too quickly. His whole mean manner was probably just part of his act. And his magic was fabulous. There's nothing worse than a bad magician, one whose tricks you can figure out. With Presto, it wasn't like that. I had no idea how he did his tricks. No idea at all.

Hector was writing again. "Ah," said Presto, "looks like our little sick friend has something new to tell us." He snapped his fingers, producing a pair of glasses out of thin air. He put on the glasses and peered at Hector's notebook, reading the message out loud. " 'Do you know Laura Bates?' "

He handed back the notebook. He put his glasses into his left fist, waved his right hand over his left, then opened both hands to show that they were empty. "Never heard of her. Why?" Something about the way he said this made me think Presto didn't get many dates. He had this nervous manner and never stopped performing and it probably turned girls off. I no longer thought Presto was up to no good. In fact, I was feeling sorry for him!

"She's going to be a guest at the party tonight," I said.

"Oh, there's hundreds of guests," said Presto. "Hundreds. So what's the deal with Laura? What's going down, as they say?"

I glanced at Hector. We were stuck with the same problem we'd had with the two painters. *Do we trust this guy? Is he a friend? Or is he one of Laura's killers?*

"We think Laura's in serious trouble," I said, deciding to trust Presto.

From the look on Hector's face, he was surprised that I'd blurted this out. He'd clearly voted for not saying anything.

"What kind of trouble?" asked the magician.

"Big trouble. Murder."

Presto turned red. He didn't say a word. And right away I felt scared—scared that I had just made a major mistake. Presto studied us, his crumply face getting even more crumply, his eyes squinting. He glanced around the car. We'd made some stops and there were two other passengers now, I was very glad to see. But Presto moved closer.

"Where'd you hear that?" he asked, his voice low.

Hector turned pale. I stammered something.

"Listen," Presto said, his voice even lower. "Let me give you a piece of advice. Don't go anywhere near this party, understand? I mean, I have to go because I gotta make a living. But Captain Blood . . . well, let's just say his parties are no place for kids. Understand? I mean, I've been performing for Blood for years. I've seen it coming. Every year his parties have been getting weirder and weirder. But tonight . . ."

"Tonight what?" I said, finding my voice again. "I mean, on the invitation there's this word with six letters but it only—"

Presto grabbed my wrist and squeezed hard, silencing me. "Listen to me!" he whispered. "Don't get on that boat. That's all I can tell you. You got it?"

"Ow! You're hurting me!" I said.

The train lurched to a halt. The doors slid open. It was our stop. Presto glared at me a second longer, then let go of my wrist and bolted off the train. Despite Presto's warning, Hector and I ran after him.

I was no longer feeling sorry for Presto.

I was feeling as if Presto was in on it.

Presto was going to kill Laura.

For a big man, Presto moved really fast. Hector and I couldn't keep up with him as we ran from the subway to the waterfront. He didn't wait for us, either. Just ran. Within two blocks we'd lost sight of him.

It wasn't hard finding our way, though. We kept seeing these eerie wooden signs—carved hands pointing the way to Pier 39. Like the invitation, the wooden hands dripped with fake blood.

It was dark out. The wind bit our faces. I smelled salt air and dead fish. Overhead I made out the shapes of dark clouds gathering like a flock of vultures. It looked as if it was going to be a dark and stormy night after all.

We were passing fewer and fewer people. On either side of us loomed big, empty-looking warehouses with dark, gaping windows. As if that weren't scary enough, we were chasing Presto, a man I now suspected was in on a murder plot.

And then I saw it.

We'd reached the pier. Up ahead, in the dark water, floated a big cruise ship. The ship was painted black. Pitch-black. If it hadn't been for the yellow lights strung along the outside of the ship and shining from the portholes, the ship would have been black as death.

THE RAVEN, said the gold letters painted on the ship's side. Up top the ship's flag showed a vicious-looking black bird. The flag flapped angrily in the wind. It looked as if the bird were trying to take off.

Hector and I walked toward the ship, but we were moving slowly. I had convinced myself that going to Laura's apartment wasn't all that dangerous. There was no way to convince myself that *this* wasn't dangerous. Walking into that black ship—it was like walking into a giant coffin.

Up ahead I could see a whole mess of parked cars. Then a cab whooshed past us in the darkness, horn blaring, tires squealing. A woman got out and ran up the gangplank to the ship.

A beautiful woman with flowing red hair.

It was as if her painting had come to life.

"Laura!" I shouted. But the cold wind blew the name back in my face. We were too late. Laura was on board.

I stopped. Stared. I had been concentrating so hard on keeping Laura from getting on this boat. Now that she was on it, I almost expected the whole ship to blow sky-high.

I started forward, but Hector got hold of my backpack, pulling me back. I tried to squirm free, but he shook his head. He growled something. I couldn't understand him.

"What?" I cried.

Instead of answering, he sneezed three times in a row. He

blew his nose. Then he held up a hand for me to wait. *Wait*? I felt like shrieking. They could be killing Laura right this instant. But I held still while Hector wrote me a note.

"2 dangerous. Wait 4 team!"

I agree, wrote Ghostwriter, flashing the letters in red on Hector's note. I sense grave danger. Grave!

"I don't care," I said, which was a big fat lie, but I was trying to convince myself for Laura's sake. "Hector, I don't believe you. I never thought you'd be a scaredy-cat."

Hector's dark eyes flashed. It was a mean thing to say, I know, and it wasn't even slightly true. But my temper was getting the better of me again.

"We have to warn Laura," I said. "C'mon, we'll get her to come off the boat. Then we can all wait on the pier together."

Still angry, Hector pushed past me and started to run. He charged up the wooden gangplank. I ran after him. Just as—

The big, dark cruise ship gave a blast on its horn so loud I nearly had a heart attack.

And as soon as we stepped on deck, two dockworkers started unhooking the gangplank behind us. I stared at them in horror. So much for my plan.

Just then there was another squeal of tires as two more cabs pulled into the parking lot at the edge of the waterfront. In the darkness I saw Alex and Gaby and Casey and Jamal and Tina and Tina's dad all piling out of the two cabs. The team started running toward the boat. I shouted. Hector waved.

Then the boat pulled out.

"Where are you going?" I heard Alex screaming.

"Come back! Come back!" yelled Mr. Nguyen.

My friends all stood at the edge of the pier, jumping up and down and waving. They were yelling at the dockworkers who had stayed on shore. But all the time, the big black boat chugged farther down the East River. As if Presto had cast an evil shrinking spell, my teammates became smaller and smaller.

Hector and I stood at the railing, gripping the wet, cold metal. I felt as if we were being taken away from our teammates forever. Maybe we were. Hector was giving me a mean I-told-you-so look. Then he started coughing.

Either the weather was getting worse, or weather is worse in the middle of a river than it is on the shore. It had gotten colder. The wind whipped drops of icy water off the river into our faces. We were both wearing shorts and T-shirts. Not exactly storm gear. And Hector was already sick.

"Now what?" Hector wrote in his notebook.

The letters disappeared as fast as he could write them. I turned to watch them go. Ghostwriter was flying the message back to shore. The pages of the notebook riffled. He was bringing the team everything we'd written, trying to get them caught up. A message came back. Hide! We'll get cops.

Hector gave me a little smile. It was as if he was teasing me with his eyes. I guess he wanted to get me back for that scaredy-cat crack. Because his look said, *Well, Lenni? Is that what you want to do? Hide?*

That was exactly what I wanted to do. But I said, "C'mon, we've got to find her."

Then I turned.

And found myself staring up at a tall, bony man in a black suit.

I've seen cartoons where Death himself comes to call for someone. This guy would have been perfect for the part. He had a bald head and a face like a skeleton. All he needed was the sickle and the black hood.

I was ready for the man to grab me, choke me, or at least yell at me for stowing away on the ship. But instead, in this strange, deep voice, the bald man said, "Good eveningggg. And welllllllcome to Captain Blooooood's boat party."

He was talking in a foreign accent and drawing out certain words like a vampire in a movie. I would have turned and run, but that would have meant diving off the boat.

The bald guy pointed to his name tag. "I'mmmm Asa Luther." He took two blank tags out of his black coat pocket. "And what are yourrrrr names?"

Hector and I looked at each other. If we said our names, would he know we were stowaways?

"Commmmme now," said Asa, "it's not that hard a questionnnn. Your names!"

I told him our names. Asa wrote them on the tags with a black waterproof marker. Then he carefully drew a skull and crossbones under each name. My heart sank down through the boat and into the bottom of the river. "What's that for?" I asked.

Asa looked up. He stared at me coldly, as if he didn't understand the question. "Just put the tags onnnn," he said. "And don't give me annnny trouble."

We did as we were told. Then Asa clapped his hands together so hard I thought his bones would snap.

"Welllll," he said, "nowwwww that we've gotten acquainted, I must be off. You're on your own unnnntil eight. Enjoy yourselves however you see fittttt. There's food, dancing. Andddd you can go exploring—but, of course, do not go into the captain's private cabin, whatever you doooo." He swiped a bony finger across his neck to show what would happen to us if we did. I gulped.

"At eight everyone will meet in the ballroom for dinner and a showwwww," he added.

Then he smiled. From most people, a smile is a good thing. From Asa . . . I gasped. His teeth were yellow and rotten and there were several black, gaping holes. He laughed when he saw how scared I was.

"Listen, uh, Mr. Luther," I began. I was so scared my voice sounded like Hector's. "We're looking for Laura Bates. I wonder if you could—"

Asa's face twisted into a mask of rage. "What? Who told you her name?"

"Uh . . . well . . . I . . ."

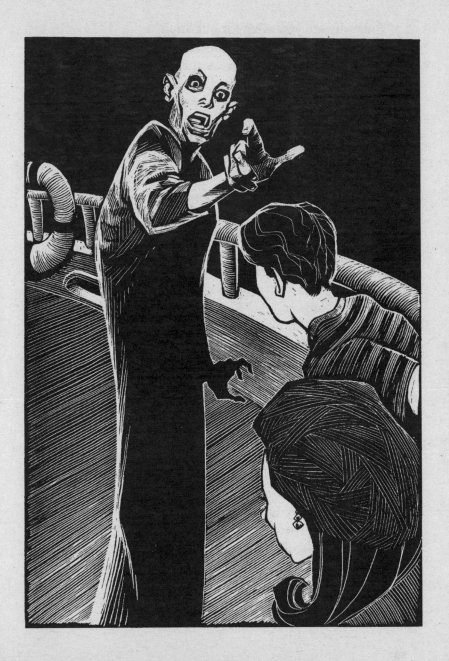

"And why are you saying it out loud?"

Hector and I backed up. Asa followed, pointing a bony finger right in my face. Then we turned and ran.

Asa ran after us. We flew down a flight of wet metal steps and burst through a set of black double doors. I kept imagining Asa's bony fingers closing around the back of my neck. We ran faster. We raced down a long, narrow corridor. Down another flight of steps. And banged through a door.

We ended up in the ship's engine room. A huge, dark, dank basement of a room with machines everywhere, hissing and clanging. Outside the metal walls of the engine room, we could hear water slap-slapping against the side of the ship.

We waited.

Asa didn't appear.

We had lost him.

"Hector," I whispered when I got my voice back, "if we get off this boat alive, you can say 'I told you so' forever."

Hector didn't smile. He wrote me a message. "Don't worry. We won't get off boat."

"You really know how to calm me down," I said.

More than anything else in life, I wanted to stay right where I was, hiding, the way the team had suggested. But Laura was somewhere on this boat. Laura was about to die.

"C'mon," I said.

Arm in arm—because we were both scared out of our minds—Hector and I made our way out of the engine room, back up to the main deck. I expected Asa to jump out and strangle me any second.

The *Raven* was a big boat. It wasn't rocking too badly. Still, it didn't feel like solid ground, either. I gripped the railing as we walked. Any second I was sure the boat was going to pitch to the side and send me flying.

On the other hand, struggling against the fast-flowing current of the river might be safer than wandering around this ship.

We came to a flight of black metal steps, slippery wet. As we struggled up to the main deck, I heard music. It was the kind of music I've heard all my life, pretty much since the cradle. Jazz. That made me feel a little better. Then I recognized the tune.

I knew the song from one of Dad's scratchy old Jelly Roll Morton LPs. It was "Dead Man Stomp."

Dancing partygoers crowded the main deck. At first glance it looked like a mass of dancing rats. Everyone was wearing black. Not just black suits, but black shirts, black blouses, black ties, black hats.

"Hector," I whispered, "just what kind of party is this?"

Hector shrugged and wrote, "Mucho strange! Looks like they R going 2 1/2 a funeral."

"Looks like they're going to have a funeral," I said, sorting out his shorthand clues. Then we both stared at each other. Whose funeral? Laura's?

Moving through the crowd with trays of food, the waiters wore black as well. I remembered that I hadn't eaten anything in hours. I waved at a waiter. He came over, holding out his tray. Even the food was black, little black rolls wrapped around globs of tiny black eggs.

"What's that?" I asked, making a face.

"Caviar," the waiter said coldly.

"Which is?"

"Fish eggs."

I gulped and shook my head. *What else are you serving?* I felt like asking. *Frog doo-doo?*

I gave Hector a questioning look, to see if he wanted some. By way of an answer, he made gagging sounds. The waiter moved quickly away.

We craned our heads around, trying to spot Laura. Or Asa. Since we were the only kids at this party, it was hard to see. Everyone was taller than we were.

Hector jumped up and down, trying to get a better look. I crossed my arms, totally terrified and totally uncomfortable. I felt as if we were wearing huge signs that said WE'RE WEIRDOS AND WE DON'T FIT IN. For one thing, we weren't wearing black. For another, we were totally underdressed. Not just for the weather but for a fancy event like this one.

When I told this to Hector he wrote, "Earrings."

At first I didn't know what he meant. I was starting to feel kind of annoyed at how short his notes were getting, like riddles. Then I got it. My hands flew to my ears. I felt the thick jewels. Sure enough, I had forgotten to take them off.

"Well, that's lucky in a way," I said, "since it means I'm dressed up, at least around the ears."

That's what I said to Hector. But what I was feeling was—*dumb*. I felt as if I'd brought my mother's spirit on board the ship—another person I'd put in danger!

I took Hector's hand and pulled him in the direction of the music. We had to say "Excuse me" about a hundred times to make our way to where the band was playing.

I've met a lot of musicians, because of my dad. I figured I might know somebody in the boat's jazz group. But when we reached the trio, I saw three unfamiliar faces. The musicians didn't smile at us, either, which musicians usually do when kids come up to the edge of the stage to listen. They stared down at us coldly, like three murderers.

We moved away. "Hector," I said quietly, "I'm beginning to get a very weird feeling about what's going on here."

"U R beginning 2 get weird feeling?" Hector wrote.

I smiled. Or tried to. Out of the corner of my eye I spotted a tiny fireball of green sparkles whizzing past. The sparkles sizzled across the invitation sticking out of a man's suit pocket, then dove down under Hector's arm and disappeared inside his notebook. Hector opened the notebook. Ghostwriter had written:

___ ___ ___ ___ E ___

Hector and I moved to the side of the ship, trying to get away from all the black-clothed guests, which wasn't easy. "Ghostwriter found this on somebody's invitation," I told Hector.

Hector snapped his fingers, then smacked his forehead. Then he held both arms out wide and said something I couldn't for the life of me understand.

"Write it!" I whispered.

"L.M.'s S diff," he wrote.

"Laura's is diff," I said, trying to translate. "Laura's what is diff? And what's diff? Hector, you're writing too fast and too short—I can't get it."

Frustrated, Hector stabbed the page with his pen, then wrote out the rest of the letters in the *diff* word: *erent.*

"*Diff-erent. Different!* Laura's is different. Got it. Her what is different? Her invitation?" Hector grinned. I pulled out Laura's invitation. He was right. The mystery word on Laura's invitation was ___ ___ R ___ ___ ___.

"And Presto's had a different letter too," I realized suddenly. I wrote it down.

___ ___ ___ ___ ___ R

"So maybe we have to combine them all," I said. But

Hector was way ahead of me. He'd already written __ __R__ER, and then he'd written a note to Ghostwriter explaining what he was doing. Right away Ghostwriter pulled three letters out of our notes and stuck them in the remaining blanks:

DARKER.

That didn't sound right. I guess Ghostwriter agreed. The letters vanished as he tried again. BURNER. And again. FARMER. By now, I was whispering guesses and Hector was writing down guesses of his own. Our teammates back on shore were sending us words, too, via Ghostwriter. Then Ghostwriter came up with HARDER and LARDER. And as he switched the letters around, he left the last four letters in place for a second: __ __RDER.

And then I had it.

Only I didn't call it out.

I just opened my mouth.

So did Hector. 'Cause we both knew the word.

So did Ghostwriter. We watched silently as Ghostwriter dropped the missing two letters into position:

MURDER.

Presto's warning rang in my ears. Captain Blood's parties had been getting weirder and weirder. But tonight . . . tonight someone at the party was planning . . .

MURDER.

We already knew that, I told myself. But it was the kind of news that scared you every time you heard it.

Hector shut his notebook. We pressed back against the railing, trying to get as far away from the party as we could. My stomach heaved. The rocking of the ship had finally gotten to me. I felt as if I was going to throw up.

"Laura," I said faintly, feeling my face turning as green as my precious earrings. "We've got to find Laura."

Just then Hector gasped and pointed behind me.

I whirled around, thinking—hoping—he'd found Laura. But that didn't make any sense, because he was pointing off the side of the ship.

Where this gigantic green woman stood, all lit up in the darkness, her proud, somber face gazing straight ahead.

I've always loved the Statue of Liberty. In fact, sometimes I've fantasized that I am the Statue of Liberty. I love the way she holds that torch up so high and proud. I love the way she's a symbol of freedom in this country. I'd never seen the statue up close, though. When you live in New York City, you end up not doing all the tourist stuff.

Right then, sailing past the statue gave me a shot of confidence. *I will be brave,* I told myself. *I will handle this. I will not chuck my cookies. Hector and I and Ghostwriter and the team—we'll find Laura and save her.*

A loudspeaker crackled to life. "Ahoy, my lily-livered landlubbers. This is Captain Blood speaking."

The band stopped. The chitchat stopped. That voice. It sounded as if the captain was chewing on glass. The voice also sounded strangely familiar.

"If you'll set your gaze starboard, mates, you'll spy that we are now passing the Statue of Liberty. Liberty. Ha! What a disgusting idea. Personally, I'd prefer a Statue of Torture. But what can you do?"

Captain Blood's sickening laugh boomed all over the boat. "And speaking of liberty, now that you're on my boat, you're all my prisoners, aren't you? Can't go anywhere. Unless of course you want to swim—and take a trip all the way down to Davey Jones's locker."

Hector and I stared at each other, our eyes widening.

Captain Blood laughed some more, until he began wheezing and coughing worse than Hector. When he was done,

he added, "I'll be pointing out more sights as we go along, mates. Cheerio." The announcement clicked off. The band started up and people began talking.

Then suddenly—

"Don't move!" a voice shouted as a man grabbed my ears.

10

"Oh, they're gorgeous! Simply gorgeous!" the man cried.

He was studying my earrings. I was studying him—as best I could. My heart was pounding.

He was short, about my height even though he looked older than forty. Like everyone else on the ship, he was dressed all in black. He had a thin body and a big head like a mushroom. His voice was high. His name tag read C. D. DIAMOND.

"Biggest emeralds I've ever seen," Mr. Diamond murmured, his eyes shining.

He whipped out a small bell-shaped magnifying glass. "You don't mind if I have a look with my loupe?" He didn't wait for my permission, just pulled my head closer as he peered at my earrings through his loupe. "Oh," he said, letting me go. He frowned. "Glass!"

Glass? What was he talking about?

He must have seen the confused look on my face because he said, "They're fake. Worthless. Not real emeralds at all. Sorry."

"That—That can't be," I stammered.

"Oh, but it can, and it is. Sorry."

Mr. Diamond smiled. Hector flashed me a sympathetic look. Good old Hector, he knew what I was going through.

It wasn't the money I cared about. The earrings have mostly sentimental value for me. But I'd always thought my mother's earrings were real. The idea that they were fakes made me sadder than I could explain.

"Oh, I've made you unhappy. I'm so, so sorry," piped Mr. Diamond in his fluty voice. "There, there, there"—he patted my cheek—"don't cry, little girl."

"I'm not going to cry. And I'm not a little girl!"

But the truth is, I felt like crying. These earrings are the one thing I have of Mom's. Mom was gone forever. And if the earrings were fake, well . . . It somehow meant she was even farther from me than before.

Hector scribbled a note. Mr. Diamond's thin eyebrows rose in a question. We both looked at what Hector had written: "Maybe he wrong. Maybe real."

"Me? Wrong?" Mr. Diamond laughed gaily, rubbing his hands together nervously. "My dear young man. You're looking at the world's foremost jewelry expert. Tip-top tippy-top tip. I've got an eye for these things. More's the pity for you, am I right? Still . . ."

He lowered his voice and leaned closer. "I'd be very careful, if I were you. Very—very—very—careful. Those earrings of yours could fool a lot of people. And Captain Blood

. . . well, let's just say he doesn't always have the finest quality of people at his parties. In fact, there are several criminal types here tonight, if you want to know the truth."

Big surprise.

"Just be careful," Mr. Diamond said. "Those earrings of yours look good enough to kill for. Ta-ta."

He vanished into the crowd.

I shivered. I was still trying to get my mind around the idea that Mom's earrings were fake. Now there was the new idea that I could get killed for wearing fake earrings.

Hector nudged me in the ribs with his notebook. "Don't worry," he'd written. "Glass, not glass, still beautiful."

I should have smiled at the compliment, but I kept frowning.

He wrote more, then nudged me again. "Put earrings back on," his new note said.

I stared at the note for a moment, puzzled. "What are you talking about? I never took my earrings off."

Suddenly I felt as if I were falling off the boat.

I reached slowly for my ears.

My earlobes were bare.

I'd been robbed!

11

"I've been robbed!" I shouted. "I've been robbed!"

I didn't mean to shout. Hector tried to cover my mouth with his hands. But it was too late. The band stopped playing. All heads turned toward us.

A crowd gathered around. Men and women dressed in black stared at me with curious, excited faces.

"Robbed? Did you say robbed?"

"What'd they get?"

"Something valuable?"

"Hey, you have any other valuables left on you?"

They were all laughing, poking at me and Hector.

Just then a tall man pushed his way through the crowd. "Pardonnnnn me, excuse me, let me throughhhhh!"

Asa.

Hector grabbed my hand and we started to run. Asa raced after us. This time we ran up the steps instead of down. And up. And up. Until we came to the bridge. Not a *bridge* bridge. This bridge was the room on the ship with the captain inside and the wheel that steers the ship—they call that the bridge.

We could see the captain. Steering the ship. And staring at us in surprise.

Captain Blood.

Not someone we figured we could trust.

We kept running. We ran around the bridge, and as Asa chased after us, we clattered back down the wet metal steps.

This time we ran around a gangway, through a set of black double doors, and into a long, narrow corridor. We flew past several doors until we came to a door marked RAVEN SECURITY.

Security! That was just what I was looking for. I had a brief image of what I hoped would be inside: a roomful of security blankets.

Hector knocked sharply on the door, then yanked it open. We practically dove inside, closing the door behind us.

Outside in the hallway there was only silence. We had lost Asa once more.

Inside, the cabin was small, with two desks facing each other. At the desks sat two security officers in uniforms. The uniforms were black, like everyone else's clothes on this ship, but with their brass buttons and insignias these officers looked official. A comforting sight.

They both stared at us openmouthed. "Can we help you?" one of the officers asked.

"I sure hope so," I said. "I was just robbed."

"Robbed?" said one of the officers, nervously pushing his black-framed glasses up his nose. His name tag said OFFICER WILL KETCHAM, CHIEF OF RAVEN SECURITY.

"Also, someone is chasing us and trying to kill us."

Officer Amanda P. Lisa Fource, a big woman with short, brown hair and a round, serious face, slapped down her Styrofoam cup. Coffee sloshed over onto her desk. "Kill you? Oh, come now."

"What was stolen?" asked Officer Ketcham, as if that was the only subject that interested him.

"M-My earrings. My mother's earrings."

My voice, I noticed, shook. I sure hoped I wasn't going to cry. I shouldn't have said that word—*mother*. That one word is more likely to make me teary than any other word in the English language.

"I know who took them, too," I added.

Hector had been writing. He held up his notebook. Officer Fource read what he'd written. "Mr. C. D. Diamond?" she asked. She reached up to a black metal shelf over her desk and pulled down a clipboard. I could see over her shoulder. The list of names she was studying was headed THE RAVEN, PASSENGER LIST. And then today's date, April 12.

Ghostwriter dashed through the list at lightning speed. Hector and I exchanged glances. The cabin had two small round portholes, like the windows on washing machines. We watched Ghostwriter's green sparkle fly off the passenger list and blast out through the left porthole. I could see the tiny green fireball zipping toward shore—and the rest of our team—like a stray firework escaped from a Fourth of July party.

Officer Fource looked up from the list, surprised. "There's no Mr. Diamond listed here."

"That means he's a stowaway," said Officer Ketcham, looking grim.

"A stowaway?" I asked. Right then I remembered that that was what we were, Hector and I. We weren't on that passenger list, either. What would these officers do to us if they found that out?

"I can't tell you how much we hate stowaways," Officer Fource said with an odd smile. She made a fist and pounded her palm with it.

"Don't worry," Officer Ketcham told me. "Bottom line is we'll find him, whoever he is. We'll get your earrings back. And then we'll throw him in the ship's brig to rot."

"The brig? What's that?"

"Ship's prison."

"Ah, prison," I said, my voice cracking. "He'll go there just for stowing away?"

"And for the robbery," Officer Ketcham said, giving me a strange look. Then he made me describe Diamond as carefully as I could. Hector drew them a picture and ripped it out of his notebook. But all the time I kept thinking about the fact that we had stowed away.

Hector and I have every right to be on this ship, I told myself firmly. I'd been so distracted by the robbery and by Asa that I'd almost forgotten what we were doing here. And how helpful these security officers could be. Never mind our safety. There was Laura to think about.

"Listen," I said. "There's something else. Something worse than earrings."

Officer Fource raised one eyebrow. "Oh?"

"You've got to help us. We think—we *know* there's going to be a murder on the ship tonight."

Both officers stared at me coldly. Then they smiled, but the smiles seemed fake.

"Now why would you say that?" asked Officer Ketcham.

"You're not starting that murder business again, are you?" asked Officer Fource. "Oh, come now, security on this ship isn't as bad as that!"

Hector held up his notebook. He'd written "Laura Bates."

"Right," I said. "Laura Bates. That's who's going to be killed."

Officer Fource checked her passenger list again. "Hmm. No Laura Bates listed, either."

"But that's impossible!" I said. I was starting to get that nightmare feeling, where you wish you could wake up so the whole strange mess would go away. But I was already awake. "Look, I—we both saw Laura go on board. I have her invitation right—"

I was about to get the invitation out of my backpack when Officer Ketcham came over and put a big hand on my arm. He wasn't gripping me as hard as Presto had on the subway, but he was holding me tight.

"Don't bother with the invitation," he said. "Believe me, you're wrong. I mean, think about it. Who would plan to commit a murder on a ship? How could the murderer ever hope to escape? That's crazy. Pure nonsense. Really." He gave me another warm smile. It chilled my blood.

Officer Fource switched on the mike that sat on her desk. "Attention, passengers," she announced. "Attention all passengers. This is Officer Fource, *Raven* Security. I'm sorry to interrupt your party, folks. But I'm afraid there's been a robbery. Looks like we've got a jewel thief on board. So please—until we catch this guy—watch your valuables closely.

"And Mr. Diamond, if you're listening, you might as well

turn yourself in right now, buddy, and save yourself a whole heap of trouble. 'Cause we're going to search this ship from top to bottom. We're going to find you, pal."

Officer Fource flicked off the mike. She smiled at me. "There you go," she said. "Don't worry. We'll find him."

Officer Ketcham opened the door. "And now," he said, "go enjoy the party. I promise you'll get your earrings back before the night is done. I mean it."

He winked.

"But what about the murder plot?" I said pleadingly. "Look, that's why that crazy man Asa is chasing us. Because he's afraid we'll tell everyone about Laura. He's in on it."

It was as if Officer Ketcham's face had turned to stone. "Asa is chasing you?"

He glanced back at Officer Fource. She gave me an odd look. "Why don't you come back in the office for a sec?" she asked us.

We had a different plan. Hector and I started to run.

"Hey! Come back here!" Officer Ketcham yelled after us.

"Stowaways!" yelled Officer Fource.

We ran until we came to a deserted railing at the back of the ship. We could see the white trail of foam the boat made as it churned through the water.

"This is bad, Hector," I said quietly.

He nodded. Suddenly he grabbed my arm. He looked scared—so scared that I got terrified. In fact, I could barely breathe. "What?" I asked. "What?"

He gasped out the words, but barely any sound came out. His voice was totally gonesville. He wrote his message in his notebook.

"What if all in on it?" I read aloud.

Then we stared at each other.

"Everyone on this ship?" I asked, my voice going up and up. "You think they're all planning to murder Laura together?"

"An interesting theory," said a voice.

We both spun around.

Standing behind us at the ship's railing was an elderly woman in a long black dress, a black knitted shawl, and a black tiara. Pearls hung from her neck, and I could see more jewels around her wrists.

"An interesting theory, but I highly doubt it." She had a merry, twinkly voice, but her beady eyes were like the eyes of a hawk that has just spotted a mouse. "You see, for a murder you must have a motive."

There was that movie business again, the thing the painters had talked about.

"There are more than two hundred guests on this ship, not counting the crew," said the old woman. "For everyone to have a motive to kill this poor Laura of yours is very unlikely, don't you think? No, no, I assure you, when the night is done there will be one, or at most two killers, working together.

"I, for instance, have a very good motive for killing someone on this ship. Care to hear it?"

12

I didn't care to hear it. But the old woman beckoned us closer. We didn't have much choice. Ghostwriter read the woman's name tag: IONA D. BANKS.

"There's a young woman on the ship tonight," said Iona, glancing around sneakily. She lowered her voice. "Her name is Vera Greta Stone. I'm sure you've heard of her."

Hector and I shook our heads.

"Oh, my little dears, you're so young, and you've so much to learn. Vera Stone is the proud owner of the most famous diamond in the world. The Gigante."

The way she said that word—*Gi-gan-te*—it was as if she were eating something delicious.

"The jewel has been handed down in Vera's family from generation to generation," said Iona. She gazed out at the dark water, as if lost in thought. "Some people are born with a silver spoon in their mouths. Vera was born with the most beautiful diamond in history." She sighed. "Rumor has it that she wears it everywhere. And that means . . ."

She turned back to us. Her eyes sparkled like evil gems.

"That means we're on board with the Gigante at this very instant."

I was seasick again. There was all this different stuff floating around in my brain—Laura, the killers, Mr. Diamond, my earrings, the robbery. I didn't have room for anything else. Let alone the most valuable gem in the world. My mouth hung open. I was in a daze.

Before tonight, the most valuable things I'd ever seen were my emerald earrings. Then I'd found out they were worthless. And here I was on board a ship with a jewel worth more money than I could even imagine.

"I used to be wealthy myself," Iona was saying. I tried to focus on her words. Used to be wealthy?

"That was before the collapse of three of my banks," she explained. Her voice dropped into despair. "Today I don't have a penny to my name."

"But—" I pointed to her jewelry.

"Glass, my dear. All glass. I try to keep up appearances." She flashed the briefest of smiles. "That's why I go to fancy functions such as this one." Another brief smile. I watched her wrinkled hands kneading the leather strap of her black purse. She was twisting the strap so hard I was sure she'd break it. "Now if I could have that diamond—," she said. "Well, to put it bluntly, I'd kill for that diamond."

Her voice spiked in volume when she said the word *kill*. Then she saw me and Hector looking at her. She smiled as if she had just remembered we were still there.

"But I probably shouldn't be telling you this, should I?"

74

she said with a bitter laugh. "If Vera shows up dead tonight, you'll go accusing me, now won't you?"

She glared at us.

"Enjoy the cruise," she said coldly.

Then she strolled off, softly humming another tune my dad likes to play: "Diamonds Are a Girl's Best Friend."

"Hector, now we have two people to warn," I said. "Laura and Vera Greta."

Hector nodded. Or maybe he just shivered; it was hard to tell. Hector looked horrible. His short, black hair was wet and shiny from the misting wind. His lips were blue. And it was all my fault.

But there was nothing I could do about that now. If we ever got off the *Raven* alive, I'd make him a gallon of chicken soup. I wrapped an arm around his shoulder and led him back down the corridor and out of the cold.

Huge gold letters hung in the air over our heads, trembling. **What is going on?**

Ghostwriter. He had taken the gold letters off the cabin doors. He was bringing a message from the team.

What was going on? That was a very good question. The way my head was spinning, it wasn't a question I could answer very well. Hector and I huddled in the corridor, using Hector's notebook to talk with our teammates.

Tina sent the first message. She suggested we write down everything we knew so far, to see if we could organize our data.

"We know we could be killed at any second," I whispered. Hector wrote this down. I was trying to suggest that this wasn't the time to make a casebook. But Hector kept writing the rest of our clues and facts.

We knew that two killers were planning to kill Laura Bates. We knew Laura was somewhere on the ship. We knew there was a magician named Presto on board who might or might not be part of the murder plot. And we knew that a man named C. D. Diamond was a jewel thief and a stowaway and that he had my earrings.

We also knew that Asa was after us. And that Captain Blood was weird.

Hector gave me a look as if he was beginning to hit overload. But he wrote down what I said.

What else did we know? We knew that the security officers seemed to be working with Asa. And that Iona wanted to kill some woman named Vera Greta.

Usually when our team makes lists like this, it helps. But this time I only felt more confused, as if my mind were turning to mush.

" 'Find Laura,' " I said, pointing to a phrase Hector had written down. That was our original plan and I didn't see any reason to change it. "C'mon," I said.

We crept down the corridor. Past black doors labeled CABIN this and CABIN that. Hector was trying all the doorknobs, knocking, too. I started softly calling Laura's name. And Vera's name. I got no answer to either one.

Then we came to the last door in the corridor. As Ghostwriter read the name on the cabin door, I turned the doorknob. This door was open. I was so surprised that I almost fell into the cabin.

Standing inside, with her back to us, was Laura.

She turned around fast.

Except it wasn't Laura. Not Laura at all. Up close, I'd only seen a painting of her. But I knew right away this wasn't Laura. For one thing, there were strands of blond hair poking out from under this woman's flowing mop of red hair. For another, this woman looked mean, not kind.

"What are you doing in here?" the young woman snapped. "This room is private!"

"Aye," rasped an old man's voice. "Private quarters, mates. I'll slit the gizzard of anyone who comes in here without a very good reason."

Sitting on the other side of the cabin was a man with a black eyepatch, a scraggly gray goatee, and a pirate's hat. He clutched a roll of mints and sucked one noisily.

"Don't just stand there gaping, you little brats," the old man snarled. "Get out before I use me cutlass on your belly!"

I was too stunned to move. Hector had to pull me out of the cabin. The young redheaded woman slammed the door in our faces. Locked it, too, hard and fast.

I was left staring at the sign on the door, which I hadn't noticed before. Ghostwriter made the words flash, trying to warn us:

CAPTAIN BLOOD, PRIVATE CABIN
KEEP OUT!

The one cabin that Asa had warned us not to go into.

But that wasn't what had me so horrified. I pushed Hector down the hall. Around the next corner, I shoved him against another cabin door. "Hector," I whispered, holding my face close to his. "It's them. It's them! It's them!"

His mouth formed the silent question, "Who?"

"The voices on the phone. An old man and a young woman. That was them! The killers!"

13

We were both shaking. And then I had another horrible thought.

"Wait a minute," I said. "We saw the captain in the bridge. Then we saw Captain Blood. They're not the same person."

Hector's jaw dropped. It wasn't just because of my news. It was because the cabin door we were leaning against flew open.

We fell into the room.

Asa pounced on us, kicking the door shut behind us. He pulled us to our feet and threw us into two chairs. He was wild-eyed.

"Please don't kill us," I begged. "We won't tell anyone that you're killers. We—"

Asa whipped a thin black leather wallet from inside his suit jacket and flipped it open. Inside was a shiny silver badge. As he held the badge out toward us, Ghostwriter zipped across the ID number, reading.

"Undercover cop," Asa said softly.

His deep voice and his foreign accent were gone. He spoke in a kind, normal voice. He no longer seemed like the scary skeleton he had been a second ago. I gaped at him in shock.

I was worse than seasick. I felt as if my whole world were turning upside down.

"W-Why didn't you tell us?" I asked.

Asa smiled gently. "That's what undercover means, Lenni. We don't go around announcing we're on the job. And also, I didn't want you involved." As he spoke he opened the cabin door. He led us back down the corridor, toward the party deck.

"Listen, this boat is no place for you," he told us as we walked.

"We know that," I said, "but we have to save Laura."

"No, that's my job," said Asa. "And the rest of my team."

Team? So there were two teams working on this case. I felt a wave of relief. Hector smiled at me. "You have partners on board?" I asked Asa. "You mean, like Officer Ketcham?"

"Uh-huh."

So that was why the security officers had pretended they didn't believe us about Laura! They wanted to protect us.

"Now I've got to ask the two of you to stay out of harm's way," said Asa. "We can't protect three people at once."

On deck the band played on. Partygoers danced. As he spoke, Asa kept glancing around—tiny flicks of his eyes from side to side, as he made sure no partygoers were eavesdropping on our conversation. I could tell that Asa was good at what he did. He'd certainly had me fooled.

"Where's Laura?" Hector wrote in his notebook.

"Don't worry about that," Asa said firmly. "You're off the case, remember? I want you two to relax."

Relax. That was something I hadn't done in a while. Not since I'd overheard those killers on the phone. But now a real grown-up cop team was on the case and was going to protect Laura. That fact did relax me. I was worn out, I realized. Cold, wet, and tired.

"Listen, I don't have much time," Asa said. "So I need you both to promise me that you'll stop snooping around. Lenni . . . ?"

The wind was driving harder, sending biting spray into our faces. The boat had turned around and was coming up the Hudson River. New York City's magnificent skyline floated slowly by on our right: a cluster of dark skyscrapers, the windows lit like jewels. Then I noticed something about those lit windows. Ghostwriter had glowed around whole bunches of them to spell out a gigantic message. Do you trust Asa?

I hesitated. Did I? I sure wanted to take Asa's advice and drop the case. But something was still bothering me. Something was stuck in my brain the way a piece of food might get stuck between my teeth.

In the skyline, the glowing window lights changed as Ghostwriter spelled out a message from the team: Hang in there. Help is on the way.

More help. More reasons to relax.

"Lenni," Asa said, taking my elbow. "Promise me."

"I—"

I was about to promise that I'd play it safe from now on when the ship's loudspeakers barked out a new message.

"Ahoy, mates. Captain Blood speaking. For those of you smart enough to check your watches every now and again, you will see that it is after eight. That means Presto the Magnificent has already begun his magic act in the ballroom. And it means you're late! So please, rush to your seats before you miss dinner as well. But don't move too fast or you'll fall to your death off the side of the ship!" He laughed happily.

"Go!" Asa said, pushing us in the right direction. "And don't worry about a thing."

There weren't too many people on deck, but everyone who was there headed toward the steps leading to the lower deck. We were swept into the flow. I turned around once to look for Asa and saw him making his way toward the stairs to the top deck. His face had changed back into its mask of evil. I turned a second time and he was gone.

We marched through a pair of black swinging doors into the ballroom—and a burst of laughter.

We looked around in shock. Round tables, each covered with a black, velvety cloth, filled the large room. Sitting around those tables, laughing their heads off, were most of the *Raven*'s guests. At the far end of the room was a big stage. A man with an orange Mohawk strutted around the stage, clutching a microphone. Presto's snide voice blasted through the room.

"Sooo, I guess you like pancakes, am I right? And ice cream? Am I correct? What am I? I'm a mind reader, right?"

Mean laughter from the crowd. Presto was talking to a guest he must have brought up onstage. Short and badly overweight, the guest was laughing as hard as anyone. But you could see he was embarrassed.

"Now I want you to hold your wallet very tightly, sir. With both your chubby little hands."

Nervous laughter from the crowd.

"That's right, Fatty," Presto said meanly. "You can't be too careful, after all. You heard about the jewel thief who stowed on board tonight, didn't you? Ohhhhhh, now, I told you to hold on to your wallet!"

The heavy man looked down with astonishment and saw that his wallet was no longer in his hands. Right in the middle of everything else that was going on, I found myself caught up in Presto's trick. *Now how did he do that?*

"Now how did I do that?" Presto asked the crowd, grinning like a shark. "It's easy, folks. I'm *Presto! The Magnificent!*"

I was back to thinking that Presto was a jerk.

I scanned the ballroom, looking for Laura, but I didn't see her. What if they'd already killed her? "Hector? You see her?"

He wrote in his notebook: "U promised Asa."

"What? I never promised," I said. "I was *about* to promise but I didn't promise."

Hector believes in sticking by your word. I like that. "Listen," I said, "how do we know Asa is telling the truth? Maybe he's not an undercover cop. Maybe he's one of the killers."

When we'd first come on the boat, I'd thought Asa seemed weird and suspicious. Maybe my first impression had been right. "U serious?" said Hector's note.

"Kind of," I said. "I don't know who to trust anymore."

That was the truth. Hector's mystery story about the British people on the island came back to me. Maybe we were reliving that story, only on a boat, and soon the partygoers would start dropping like flies.

"Who knows? Maybe I'm the killer," I said aloud.

Hector gave me a little smile, then crossed his eyes to show he thought I was crazy. I laughed.

Hector pulled me toward a side table lined with little folded place cards. The cards said the guests' names on the outside, complete with those skulls and crossbones and more dripping blood. Inside each card someone had written a tiny black number. The table number.

"Good thinking," I told Hector. "If Laura's card isn't on this table, we know she took it, and that means she's here in the ballroom."

There weren't too many cards left, since most of the guests had already sat down. No Laura. I felt my heart pounding. She was here. I stared around the ballroom, searching for her among the guests. But it was such a big room . . .

Hector nudged me. Back on the card table, Ghostwriter was zooming from card to card, reading the names. Then he flew into Hector's notebook and wrote out the list. He made the first letter of each last name glow in a different color:

*A*dams, *A*rkin, *B*arker, *B*eattie, *B*loch . . .

Hector pointed to the glowing letters.

"The names are alphabetical," I said. "So? How does that help us?"

Then Ghostwriter started glowing on the table numbers next to the names. The Bs all seemed to be at Table 29.

Now I understood what Ghostwriter was up to. "Right! Laura must be at Table Twenty-nine with the other Bs."

Hector scribbled, "But security says no Bates listed!"

I'd been looking for Laura all day. I wasn't giving up that easily. I craned my head around, looking for Table 29. When I spotted it, I didn't see any redheads. Hector was right.

I looked back at him. He was studying the cards. He pointed his pen at a card for Mr. Leonard Slotking. Table 17. I didn't get what he was driving at.

"Vera Greta Stone," he wrote in his notebook. He underlined the *S* that started her last name and the *S* in *Slotking*.

"Yeah," I said. "Maybe that's where Vera is sitting." I wasn't excited. I guess I didn't have room in my heart to save a whole lot of people. I'd never met Vera, but ever since I'd seen that painting of Laura, I'd felt as if I'd known her all my life. I wanted to save Laura, not Vera.

Hector was already making his way toward Table 17. I followed. "Hector," I said quietly. "No."

But he didn't hear me, or he didn't listen, because he kept making his way closer to the stage, and closer to Presto, closer to Table 17.

I followed him. Then I stopped. There at Table 17, with her face turned toward the stage, was a redheaded woman. Her hair shined like copper.

I watched as Ghostwriter glowed on the woman's name tag. I was holding the notebook. So I saw his message first: **Vera Greta Stone.**

I groaned. That hair was just like the hair in Laura's painting. For one second, I'd been sure we'd found her.

Hector was almost at the table. I was right behind him. From this distance I could see the plain silver chain that Vera wore around her neck. Just as Iona had said, she wore a single diamond. Big. Sparkly. Like hundreds of tiny flashbulbs going off at once. Sure looked like the Gigante. The most valuable diamond in the world.

The woman was leaning her head on her hand, so I couldn't see her face. Then she put her hand down.

My jaw dropped.

Laura!

14

"Laura!" I gasped, without even thinking.

She looked up at me, startled. So I knew I was right. It was Laura.

Her sad eyes smiled. "Do I know you?" she whispered.

Hector was writing her a note. "I'm Lenni," I said, as if that explained anything. "And this is Hector Carrero, and we've been looking for you for hours. But—"

I had about a million things I wanted to say, and another million things I wanted to ask. I wanted to tell Laura everything that had happened. About the phone call. About going to her apartment. About Asa turning out to be an undercover cop. About Iona and her motive for killing Vera. All of which led to my most important question. Just who was this woman, exactly? Laura? Or Vera?

Before I could say a word, a loud, nasty, familiar voice bellowed, "Young lady! Do you have any idea that someone is trying to perform a magic act up here? Helloooo!"

Mean laughter from the crowd. I glanced up at the stage and saw Presto glaring down at me with that big, crumply face. I turned bright red.

"That's right, I mean you. Now sit! And shush!"

Hector and I sat in a hurry. We sat at Laura's table, but the only available chairs were across the table from her.

Presto was doing a rope trick. "I mean, cut me a little slack, why don't you?" he said. As he said the word *cut* he hacked at the rope with a huge pair of scissors. "Kids today," he muttered. He unfurled the cut-up rope. It was still in one piece. Loud applause.

Everyone at our table was watching Presto's magic act, but a few people carried on quiet conversations as well. The man on Laura's right was whispering something to her. I leaned forward and caught a little of it. At first it sounded as if the man was talking about murdering someone. Then I realized he was telling Laura the idea for a murder mystery.

"That's great," Laura answered. I could tell she didn't mean it, just wanted to make the man feel good. I beamed at her like a maniac. Luckily she didn't notice.

"You working on anything new?" the man asked Laura.

"Yeah. I've got a new idea I'm really excited about."

"What is it?"

Laura blushed. "Well, I'd tell you, but Mr. Poe says I shouldn't tell anyone. He says someone will steal it for sure."

The man next to Laura kept talking to her. As she listened, Laura gazed at the stage. But she also threw me and Hector these little smiles, signaling that she'd talk to us as soon as she got the chance.

After a day of searching for her, my heart was pounding

as if we were sitting with a movie star. I had to remind myself to close my mouth. I had figured that whoever painted Laura's portrait might have exaggerated how pretty she was. I was wrong. She was even better-looking in person. From her green almond eyes to the sparkling buttons on her neatly buttoned button-down shirt, everything about Laura gleamed and shined. The diamond around her neck was so large and shiny, I could barely take my eyes off it.

It wasn't just that I was so close to Laura. I was also close to the most valuable gem in the world.

But if Laura owned the Gigante, why was she living in that dump in Fort Greene?

And then, all at once, I had it. I looked at Hector. He was writing. I think he figured it out at the same time.

"MayB Laura hired 2 B fake Vera as way 2 protect Vera 2-night," he wrote.

I nodded. That was just what I was thinking. Laura probably couldn't afford to turn down a job, no matter how dangerous. That would explain why Asa had gotten so upset when we'd used Laura's real name. We had almost blown her cover.

But then I had another horrible thought. The killers had talked about killing Ms. Bates. So they knew they were going to kill Ms. Bates, not Vera Greta. They didn't care! Vera Greta, Laura—it was all the same to them.

And the motive those painters had hounded me about?

The Gigante diamond.

Something made me look behind me. I jumped.

Iona sat at the next table. She wasn't looking at me; she was staring right at Laura's neck.

So was the man sitting next to Iona. The man in the black eyepatch. Captain Blood.

There was a round of applause as Presto finished another trick. Captain Blood finally took his eyes—I mean his eye— off Laura and rose slowly to his feet.

"Presto, if I can interrupt for just one second . . ."

"Of course, O Captain," said Presto, bowing and scraping.

"Good evening, mates," said the captain, nervously tugging on his gray goatee. "I just have a few brief announcements."

Why don't you tell them about your little murder plot? I wanted to scream.

Instead, Captain Blood popped another mint into his mouth, which made it a little hard to understand what he was saying. "I'm sure you'll all want to hear about the vittles. The cook tells me that you have a choice tonight between linguine with garlic sauce and pepper steak. Now don't worry. We've changed cooks since our last sea voyage, so I truly doubt we'll have any more guests dying of food poisoning, ha ha.

"We are honored to have the great Presto performing for us tonight. As I'm sure you'll agree, he's not just magnificent, he's funny, too. In fact, the last time he performed, several guests laughed themselves to death, ha ha ha!"

An old waiter, a short man with a big head of fluffy white hair, a white handlebar mustache, and a deep voice, began taking dinner orders at our table. I stared at him. So did Hector. Something about him looked awfully familiar.

"And now," said Captain Blood with an eerie grin, "let's get on with what promises to be a killer of an act. Presto?"

"Thank you, sir."

As Presto started his next trick, I scribbled a note on a napkin and passed it to Laura.

"Stop pretending to be Vera. Someone is plotting to kill you for the Gigante."

Ghostwriter read the message before I passed it. Hector started writing him a note so that Ghostwriter would know what was going on. Meanwhile, Laura carefully unfolded my napkin, and I saw her blush. *Bull's-eye,* I thought. Hector and I were right.

Laura took out a pen and wrote a note underneath mine. She reached across the table to hand back the napkin.

"I know about the killers, but what Can I do? I was hired to to a job. I've got to do it."

I looked at her, stunned. She gave me a smile and a shrug.

Before I could write another note, Presto called for a volunteer. Lots of hands shot up, but Presto ignored them.

"What a bunch of schoolchildren," he said. He raised his own hand, mimicking the audience. " 'Oh, me me me me,' " he begged. " 'Pick me!' Well, no way I'm going to pick one of you brownnosers. I'm taking somebody who didn't raise his hand."

He scanned the audience, then pointed right at Laura. "You!" he shouted.

Laura blushed deeply. Smiling, she rose to her feet.

I felt an icy tingle race over my body. "Don't go!" I warned her.

The guests at our table looked at me in surprise. There were smiles and laughs.

Laura waved at me—a wave that said "I'll be fine." She headed for the stage. Presto reached down to pull her up. She lost her balance, and he gave her a big hug as if he were trying to keep her from falling. But behind her back he winked at the audience, and got another big laugh.

He led Laura to the center of the big, dark stage. I leaned forward, ready to bolt onto the stage if Laura needed me.

Relax, I told myself. This was probably the safest Laura would be during the entire voyage. After all, she was onstage where everyone could see her. What could happen to her?

"Okay," said Presto, "for my next trick I'm going to make this lovely lady disappear."

15

Presto snapped his fingers and a large brass birdcage flew down onto the stage. He opened the front door of the cage with a huge wooden key. "Now, Vera, if you will be so kind as to step inside this cage."

I jumped to my feet. "Don't do it, Laura—I mean, Vera!"

Laughter from the crowd. My cheeks burned. Presto turned his big bulldog face slowly toward me. " 'Don't do it'?" he repeated icily.

Hector stood at my side, which gave me the courage to keep talking. "Please, Presto," I begged him. "Don't make her disappear. Let me go in her place!"

I felt very close to tears, though I couldn't tell you why.

"Now, this is what I like to see," Presto told the crowd. "A girl who really believes in magic. You really think I'm going to make Vera vanish, don't you?" he asked me. "You think she'll be gone forever, don't you?" He grinned. "Well, you're *right*! That's exactly what's going to happen!"

He whirled around, hand in the air, pointing and shouting at Laura, "Get in the cage! Now!"

Laura obeyed.

"Now, before we go any further, Vera," said Presto, talking calmly again, "I must ask you to remove your jewelry, or you'll break my magic transporter machine." He held out a hand. "The necklace."

Laura reached behind her neck, undid the clasp, and handed Presto the world's most valuable diamond.

I didn't realize what I was saying until after I said it. "Vera, it's a trick!" I yelled.

That brought down the house. Presto didn't even bother to respond, just glanced at the audience and rolled his eyes. He got another laugh.

"Now I'll take this necklace and put it in this black velvet box for safekeeping. I'm going to leave the box right here on this pedestal in plain sight. Just in case anyone gets suspicious."

He glared at me. Another laugh. Then he headed toward the cage. He gave it a hard spin.

When it stopped spinning, Laura was gone.

There was a gasp from the crowd.

"No!" I yelled. "No!"

More laughter.

Presto spun the cage again. And Laura magically reappeared.

More applause. My heart went back to beating. Presto used the big key to reopen the cage and helped Laura out.

"Now if you'll just open that little black case," Presto told her, "you can have your necklace back."

Laura walked over to the pedestal. Picked up the case. Smiled at Presto. He grinned back at her falsely, nodding for her to open it. She opened the case.

Empty.

Laura swooned. I started toward the stage. Hector right beside me. Presto caught Laura. "Vera, Vera, Vera," he said, "you're as bad as those two little brats. You think the stuff I do is real? Come now, don't you trust me? It's all a trick."

I had my hands on the edge of the stage, ready to climb up and come to Laura's defense. She was blushing as red as her hair. "S-Sorry," she stammered. "You took me by surprise. But where—?"

Presto started grunting and making other strange noises. "Excuse me," he said. "I think I've got something stuck in my teeth. Anyone have any dental floss?"

Slowly, link by link, Presto pulled Laura's necklace from his mouth. And—*plop!*—out popped the Gigante. This earned him his biggest round of applause yet.

"Gross!" I yelled, getting another huge laugh. I was becoming a regular part of Presto's act.

Breathing more easily, Hector and I made our way back to our table. Laura returned a second later, once again wearing the diamond necklace around her neck on its plain gold chain.

She smiled at me.

I froze.

Gold chain? That chain used to be silver. Presto must have—

I was about to shout out that Presto was a thief when Iona beat me to it. She leaped to her feet, pointed to the stage, and yelled, "He switched necklaces!"

I caught a glimpse of Laura as she looked at her necklace and turned red all over again. Then—

"Presto stole the Gigante!" Iona shouted. "He's a thief! Catch him! Catch him! Catch him!"

Presto leaped from the stage and raced up the center aisle with a thunderous clatter of footsteps.

"Catch him, mates! Catch him!" roared Captain Blood.

I saw Officer Ketcham and Officer Fource start after Presto, followed by a whole bunch of guests. Followed by more guests. Followed by Hector and me. There was such a crowd pouring down the center aisle it was hard to move.

We spilled out onto the main deck. By now it was pitch-dark and pouring cold rain. "There he goes!" someone shouted, pointing.

Presto was climbing up the metal ladder to the bridge, hand over hand as fast as he could go. The two security officers were right behind him. Presto raced across the bridge. There was a gasp from the crowd as Presto crashed into the captain—or whoever it was up there steering the boat.

The captain went down. The wheel spun. So did the boat.

We were all screaming now as the security officers chased Presto out the other side of the bridge. They had him cornered by the railing. Except that Presto climbed onto the bridge roof and started making his way across to the other side in the rain.

Before he could get there, Officer Ketcham dove and tackled him. They wrestled. Officer Fource jumped on top. All three of them wrestled.

My heart was in my throat. There wasn't much room up there. They were like three angels dancing on the head of a pin. Well, two angels and one thief.

Presto got up first. Officer Ketcham tried to hold his feet, but Presto kicked, and the officer went flying—

Right off the roof. Right off the boat.

There was a terrible silence from the crowd below.

Now Fource and Presto fought alone. I leaped up and tried to catch the bottom rung of the ladder, but someone in the crowd held me back.

Then I saw it. Officer Ketcham hadn't gone overboard. He was dangling off the roof of the bridge. He managed to pull himself back onto the roof. He came at Presto from behind. *Boom!* He knocked Presto down. Ketcham rode Presto's chest like a bear, while Fource snapped on handcuffs in front.

Then Officer Fource pried open one of Presto's fists. She held her hand up in triumph and shouted down to the crowd below. "It's the Gigante!"

We all cheered and clapped as if they had just performed another magic trick. We watched as the trio made their way back down to the deck. It was slow going because they had to help Presto down the ladder, now that he was wearing handcuffs.

Back on deck, Presto stood with his head bowed, his orange Mohawk matted with rain. The crowd cursed him, calling him a thief—and worse. I almost felt sorry for him.

"We're sorry for the disturbance," Officer Ketcham told the crowd. "But the important thing is, we've caught the jewel thief, and now we can return everyone's valuables and enjoy the rest of tonight's festivities."

"Yeah, check and see if he has my watch!" someone accused.

"And my brooch!" someone else yelled.

Hector and I made squinched-up faces at each other, as if we were both saying "Huh?" Because Presto was definitely not the man who'd stolen my earrings. It looked as if there were two jewel thieves on board.

Just then Iona D. Banks made her way through the

crowd. She barged right up to Officer Fource. "Let me see," she demanded, whipping out a loupe. She studied the large diamond in Officer Fource's hand. She looked up, horrified.

"This isn't the Gigante. It's a fake!" she shrieked. "Worthless glass."

Suddenly I got a very bad feeling. I looked around for Laura but didn't see her. And where were Asa and his team?

"Hector," I said, "do you see—"

Before I could finish, we heard a horrible scream from the ballroom.

We raced into the ballroom, where—

Asa stood onstage. Something about his face upset me horribly. I started walking closer, closer. Soon I was close enough to see that Asa was in tears.

Propped up next to him on metal stands were two large, colorful wooden boxes. Put together, the two boxes would be about the size of a coffin.

Standing next to Asa, looking very pale, were Captain Blood and the old waiter.

I had almost reached the stage. "What?" I demanded. "Asa! What?" Asa ignored me. As the crowd filed in, he stepped up to Presto's microphone. "Ladies and gentlemen, I'm afraid I have some explaining to do, and some terrible news. I'm an undercover cop. There are several of us on board tonight. You see, we had a tip that someone would try to steal Vera's Gigante. Well, while you were all on deck chasing Presto, I realized that Vera wasn't in the crowd. I came down here looking for her."

I felt faint. Hector held me up.

"I found these two gentlemen alone in the room," Asa said, gesturing at Captain Blood and the old waiter with disgust.

"I was finishing serving dinner," insisted the old waiter.

"I'm an old sailor," said Captain Blood, his single eye shifting back and forth. He popped another mint. "I couldn't go out in that storm. I'd catch me death o' pneumonia."

Asa ignored them. "And then I found Vera—"

He walked over to the two colorful wooden boxes and let down the flaps on the sides.

Which meant we could see what was inside the boxes.

Laura.

Sawed in half.

I was sobbing. I didn't know when I'd started sobbing, but I was sobbing now. I had tried so hard to save Laura. I didn't even know her, but— Hector had to give me a long hug before I could stop crying.

The rest of the guests had filed back into the ballroom, dripping wet, their black clothes dark and shiny.

"It's the old waiter!" someone called out. "He's the killer. I caught him trying to steal my cuff links when he served me my soup!"

"He killed Vera for the diamond!" someone else yelled.

"It's Captain Blood!" shouted another guest. "Same motive."

"It's Iona Banks!" yelled a third voice. "She's been bragging all night about how she's going to steal that diamond."

"Fool!" Iona shouted back. "I was with all of you on deck when the murder took place. How stupid can you be!"

"She's right!" another guest chimed in. "It's got to be one of these two, the waiter or the captain. Asa said he found them alone in here."

"What about Asa?" someone else called. And to my amazement and horror, there was laughter. What kind of animals were these people?

I climbed up onstage. Hector tried to stop me, but I shook him off. I had to see for myself.

A crowd had gathered around the boxes onstage, gawking like rubberneckers at a car accident. I wiped the back of my hand hard across my nose, sniffling. Not one of these jerks cared about Laura.

The crowd was still yelling out guesses about who the killer was. Hector and I had to work hard to get close enough to the boxes to see inside.

When we made it to the front, I turned away. "I can't look," I said, my voice catching.

Hector looked. I peeked.

We were looking at the box that contained the top half of Laura. When I saw her, I started crying all over again. Hector started crying too. Laura had this horrible bug-eyed look on her face, as if she'd been about to scream when she died.

"We still haven't figured out the motive," said a guest. "Presto stole her diamond. So what did the killer want?"

"The diamond Presto stole was a fake," Iona reminded us.

"What if Vera still had the Gigante hidden on her person?" someone suggested.

The gawkers surged forward, pressing Hector and me up against the boxes. They probably wanted to rip Laura's clothes off so that they could find the diamond and get rich.

"Don't push!" I shouted.

Hector grabbed the box with both hands, bracing himself. Then I saw his eyes widen. And then he started fumbling for his notebook and pen.

"Her collar!" he wrote, writing so hard and fast that his pen ripped through to the next page.

While Ghostwriter read his message, I forced myself to take another look in the box. And right away I saw what Hector was so excited about. Laura was wearing a button-down shirt. Before, at the table, all the sparkly buttons had been neatly buttoned. But now—

One wing of the collar stuck up in the air.

I started yelling. When I had the crowd's attention, I said that Vera must have used the Gigante as one of her collar buttons, as a way of hiding it. "The thief must have figured that out, too," I said. I gave the captain and the old waiter a withering stare. They both looked back blankly. "So," I said. "That solves the motive problem. Whoever the thief was, he killed Vera to get the jewel."

"Sounds about right," agreed Asa.

"One of the killers was Captain Blood," I said. "I recognize his voice. I heard him on the phone plotting this whole thing."

"I deny it, mate," Captain Blood said with a happy smile. "I deny it entirely."

"That's no proof," someone called.

"Okay. So then we should search both suspects," I said. I wanted to do a lot more to the suspects than just search them. I wanted to run at them and scratch their eyes out.

"Good idea," Asa said. "And since someone here is calling me a suspect, I volunteer to be searched as well."

Several guests stepped forward, offering to do the searching. So did Officers Ketcham and Fource.

"This is absurd," Captain Blood exclaimed, his good eye blinking furiously as a guest went through his pockets. "I'm captain of this ship. Stop it! Unhand me, you slob! Why, I've never been treated so rudely in my life! You, Ketcham, you're fired, do you hear me? Fired! Not only that, I'll slit your gizzard with me cutlass!"

"Yes, sir," said Ketcham grimly.

Every now and then, Hector and I joined in the search, when we spotted something that the searchers were missing—like the cuffs on Asa's pants. I was still crying. I could feel the tears leaking down my cheeks. But it was as if I'd stopped crying inside. Instead I felt cold anger. I breathed through my mouth.

"Hector," I whispered, "it's a good thing you have a cold."

He gave me a puzzled look.

"You can't smell. All three of these guys stink of garlic."

Several guests, overhearing my crack, started giggling like three-year-olds. Was I the only one with any respect for Laura's dead body?

So far the search had turned up nothing. The old waiter was about to rebutton his shirt when I noticed some little lumps in his ratty old T-shirt. "Pull up that shirt," I ordered him.

"No way," he said.

So two guests pulled up the shirt for him. Sewn into the underside of the shirt were all these pockets and Velcro loops. Hanging from the loops and hidden in the pockets were three watches, four pairs of cuff links, two brooches, and three pairs of earrings. One of the pairs of earrings was emerald green. They were mine.

"I thought he looked familiar!" I said, studying the old waiter more closely. Hector was looking at him closely, too, and now he reached out and yanked the man's white mustache. Luckily, Hector's hunch was right. The mustache was fake and came off in his hand.

It seemed so long since that strange little man with the high voice had stolen my earrings. I had forgotten all about—

"Mr. C. D. Diamond!" I cried.

"Yes, that's right, I'm C.D.," he confessed. "And I-I-I admit I took a few little items here and there." He was back to speaking in his real voice, high and fluty. "But I had to, uh, borrow these items, because . . . because the guests on these stinking boat parties never leave me any tips."

"Ha!" said Officer Ketcham. "No wonder we couldn't find the man you described, Lenni. He disguised himself as the waiter. Well, okay, folks, let's get this jewelry back where it belongs."

As Ketcham handed back the stolen goods, Officer Fource said, "The bad news is, we didn't find the Gigante on either one of 'em. Any more ideas, Lenni?"

Officer Fource looked very puzzled. Which was how I felt.

So it was a relief to see Hector scribbling away in his notebook. He was obviously on to something. I looked over his shoulder. He'd written, "Y does C.B. ½ garlic b.?!"

That message made no sense to me. Ghostwriter's green glow zipped through the words, reading. There was a pause. Then the glow zipped through the words again. I guess Ghostwriter was confused, too.

So was the rest of the team when Ghostwriter brought them Hector's message. The message that Ghostwriter brought back was: **Huh?**

Hector grunted in frustration, shook out the cramp in his writing hand, and started writing again.

This time he wrote out everything he was thinking. It took longer, but when he was done, the message was clear. I looked up at Officer Fource.

"We know who the real killer is," I said. "And where he's hidden the diamond!"

18

"The killer," I said, "is—"

The loudest whirring sound I've ever heard cut me off. It sounded like a giant bird flapping right over our heads.

"Attention, *Raven*!" blasted a megaphoned voice, "this is the Coast Guard. We are boarding. Repeat. We are boarding!"

"What the—?" asked Captain Blood.

Five Coast Guard officers in white uniforms burst into the room. Followed by a bunch of cops in blue. Followed by a group of kids who started barging through the crowd as they ran for the stage. Gaby, Alex, Casey, Jamal, and Tina.

"Who's this?" Asa asked as the team crowded around me and Hector.

"Friends," I said. Tina put an arm around my shoulder.

Casey took my hand. Even in the middle of all the awful stuff that was going down, it cheered me to see the team. It always does.

A moment later, we were joined onstage by Tina's father. Mr. Nguyen looked very worried. The cops swarmed around the two boxes that contained Laura's body. One cop barked into his walkie-talkie.

"There's a helicopter flying over your head and there's two choppers cruising around the boat in circles," Jamal told Captain Blood. "So don't even think about trying to escape."

"Why would I want to escape?"

"Because you're the killer," said Alex.

"How do you know?" a guest called. "You weren't even here."

"We've all been working on this mystery together," I explained, which just made everyone more confused, I could tell. But luckily Gaby started talking, explaining the solution that Hector and Ghostwriter and the team had just come up with.

"Captain Blood has garlic breath," said Gaby. "But he shouldn't have garlic breath at all, because he's sucking on a mint. Except it's not a mint. It's the—"

Captain Blood tried to swallow his mint. Tina slapped him on the back and the mint popped out onto the floor. Several guests dove onto the rolling mint as if it were a loose football in the Super Bowl. Iona came up with it. She studied it with her loupe. "It's the Gigante!"

"Murderer!" I screamed. I rushed at Captain Blood, but Tina and Jamal got in the way and held me back.

The cops started toward Captain Blood. "You're under arrest," said one burly officer. "For the murder of—"

But before he could finish his sentence, Captain Blood

removed his eyepatch. There was a perfectly good eye blinking underneath. Then he pulled off his scraggly gray goatee. Then he stepped forward and said into the microphone, "Ladies and gentlemen, looks like we have a winner."

To my confused amazement, all the guests in the ballroom started smiling and clapping and cheering.

19

"Winner?" asked Jamal. "What do you mean?"

Presto slipped out of his handcuffs and snapped his fingers. An envelope magically appeared in his hands. He grinned. "You guys solved the murder mystery, so you win the prize. A two-hundred-dollar gift certificate at Crime-time, one of New York City's finest murder mystery bookshops. Congratulations to all of you, and happy reading!"

There was a big "Oooooo!" from the crowd.

I took the envelope, but my hands trembled and I couldn't open it. I was too confused to speak. Captain Blood pulled off his black wig. He was bald underneath.

"Officers, I'm afraid these kids stumbled into our murder mystery party," said Blood. He was speaking softly now—

no more angry pirate voice. "These kids solved a murder, but not a real one."

I turned slowly toward the two boxes with Laura inside. Presto snapped the boxes together. Then he fumbled with a few latches. A minute later, Laura sat up and waved. More applause. I felt like crying all over again, this time because I was so relieved.

"But . . . but the fight, on the roof of the ship," I said, looking at Officer Ketcham. "You almost got killed."

"Oh, not at all," he said, grinning modestly.

"Bob Gold is a trained stuntman," Captain Blood said, both eyes shining. "So is Sally here. They're two of the best."

Officer Fource unbuttoned her security uniform, revealing street clothes underneath.

I turned slowly, catching glimpses of the sheepish faces on my teammates, all watching me. My head swam. I couldn't get a grip on what was happening. "So then . . . it was all made up?" I asked.

There was laughter. Laughter from the crowd of people in black. All of whom, I now understood, were mystery lovers. So that was why they all dressed and acted so weirdly. A whole boat full of people with mystery-itis.

"Ladies and gentlemen," Captain Blood said to the guests, "we've clapped for the winners, but let's also give a round of applause to our actors. David Marx, in the role of Asa—"

Asa stepped forward and bowed. Applause. Captain Blood went on to introduce the actors who had played C.D., Iona D. Banks, and Officers Ketcham and Fource. Then he said, "And you know me, of course. I'm Ed Poe."

Where did I know that name from?

"And this—"

He held out a hand toward Laura. She walked over to him shyly. "This is a star mystery-writing student of mine about whom I'm sure you'll all hear a lot more someday. Let's have a big hand for tonight's murder victim, Laura Bates!"

Right! Her teacher. Ed Poe. The painters had told us about him. Every piece was falling into place. And my embarrassment was growing. *I may blush for the rest of my life,* I thought.

"Hey, kid," Presto said to me. "I'm sorry if I scared you on the subway. I thought you kids knew this was a murder mystery game. I was just playing along."

"Me too," the actor who'd played C.D. told me. His real voice was neither high nor low. "By the way, I do know a little about jewelry. Those earrings of yours are real emeralds."

More good news. But again I got the feeling that something was missing. Something still floated loose in my head.

"Let me add my apology to the others," Officer Ketcham said kindly. "That's part of our job, to mislead anyone who comes to us during the party asking for information about the murder."

"You confused us with all that talk about Laura," Asa said, laughing. "I was afraid you were going to ruin the game!"

"Thank you for trying to save me," Laura said, giving me a smile that almost made everything better.

"Wait a minute!" I said. "None of this explains the phone call!"

The cops gave me angry looks. So did the Coast Guard officers. Even my teammates looked doubtful. No one was in the mood for any more of my theories, I could tell. But I rushed on.

"That's how we got onto this case in the first place. Our phone lines were crossed this afternoon. I heard you plotting to kill Laura," I said to Poe.

He laughed heartily.

"Well, how do you explain it?" I demanded.

"When was this?" he asked.

I had to think about that. So much had happened. The phone call seemed like last year sometime. Hector wrote down the answer. "Around four," I said.

"Ahhh," said Ed Poe, the light dawning. "There was a last-minute cancellation by the actress who usually plays Vera Greta. Ms. Bates, a student of mine, kindly agreed to fill in. You probably heard me calling in the good news."

"But you said Laura would die tonight," I said, feeling my last clue slipping away.

Ed Poe winked. "And so she did. She died. As Vera Greta."

Tina made a face. "Vera Greta? That's kind of a strange name, isn't it?"

Alex said, "Sounds a little like—"

"Very great!" said Gaby, finishing his sentence.

"Very Great Stone!" said Casey, clapping her hands. Casey loves riddles. She's good at them, too. "Her name is a joke," Casey explained to everyone onstage, " 'cause she's the character who has the big diamond."

"Exactly," said Ed Poe. The way he said it wasn't any big compliment, though.

But now the team was on a roll, working out the rest of the name clues. C. D. Diamond sounded like See the Diamond. Iona D. Banks sounded like I Own the Banks. And Asa Luther sounded like A Sleuther. Which was his role.

"Will Ketcham—will catch 'em," I muttered, massaging my head. I was getting a giant headache all of a sudden. "And Amanda P. Lisa Fource—I'm on the police force. Oh, boy . . ."

Hector gave me a look. It didn't matter that he'd lost his

voice. I could tell what he was saying just perfectly: *Boy, am I embarrassed.*

Me too, Hector, me too, I thought.

Tina's father talked with the police officers, apologizing for all the trouble we'd caused. And right about then there was a blast of the ship's horn. Followed by a PA announcement from the real ship's captain, the man we'd seen in the bridge. Captain Andersen announced that our trip had come to an end and thanked everyone for playing the *Raven* Murder Mystery Game.

"You see," said Captain Andersen, "I told you we'd get you back before eleven, and we did."

Hector and I must have gotten on board the ship too late to hear Captain Andersen's first announcement, introducing the murder mystery game. Sure would have saved us a lot of trouble if we'd arrived in time.

"Anyway," said Captain Andersen, "I hope you've enjoyed tonight's cruise, and that you'll tell your friends about us. We sail every Friday, Saturday, and Sunday night. Group rates are available."

Too late, Captain Andersen, I thought. I'd already told all my friends about the *Raven*. I'd also told the police.

I looked for Laura. But she was gone. With all the guests milling around and all the confusion, I'd lost her again.

"C'mon," Mr. Nguyen said to us, "we'd better get home."

I nodded and said, "I'd like to say goodbye to Laura."

Mr. Nguyen frowned. "Lenni, I'm sorry, but it's very late. Your dad is probably worried sick by now. And Hector looks quite sick himself. I'm afraid I must say no."

I hung my head. I couldn't argue. A minute later we were all trooping out with the rest of the guests. The boat had docked. The gangplank was back in place. I kept looking for Laura. That seemed like all I ever did anymore—look for Laura, look for Laura. As usual, I couldn't find her. What else was new?

Everyone poured off the boat, heading for their cars, heading home. The team was silent. This had never happened to us before, not since Ghostwriter had first started writing to us. A crime case had turned out to be no case at all. We'd been wasting our time—and everyone else's. All because of me.

"Laura!" someone shouted.

I stopped short. Which meant several people bumped into me from behind. I spotted who was shouting Laura's name. Captain Blood—I mean, Ed Poe. He stood at the ship's front railing. He was looking down into the parking lot.

I turned. In the darkness I saw Laura, about to get into a cab. I felt a pang. I wanted to run over to her and say I was sorry for any trouble I'd caused. But there was no way. A big crowd blocked my way.

"Don't forget your writing assignment!" Ed Poe called.

"I won't!" Laura called back. "I'm going straight home to work on it."

She disappeared into the cab. *Slam* went the door. The cab took off with a squeal. Laura was gone.

And a minute after that, we were all standing around in the rain, trying to find two cabs of our own.

It's over, I told myself. But I had the weirdest feeling.

It was a feeling I should have been getting used to.

I'd had it all day.

I felt as if Laura Bates was about to be murdered.

20

"Lenni," Mr. Nguyen said firmly, "in the cab. Now."

"Please, can't we wait and take the next one? I only need a minute."

I couldn't help it. Something felt wrong. I just couldn't put my finger on it. "Hector," I said. "Let me see the notebook."

The team gathered around me as I flipped through the pages. Thanks to his laryngitis, Hector had kept great records of our adventure. There were notes from the whole day, notes that helped me remember everything that had happened. But the rain was coming down hard. It spattered the ink, so it was a race to read Hector's notes before they disappeared.

"I hope you know what you're doing," Alex said softly,

looking over my shoulder, " 'cause Mr. Nguyen looks like he's about to have a hissy."

I barely heard him. I had just realized one of the things that was bothering me. "Wait a minute. Laura said she was going home," I said to Hector. "Right? Isn't that what she said? 'I'm going home.' "

" 'I'm going straight home,' " Tina corrected me.

"Which is what we should be doing," grumbled Mr. Nguyen.

Hector grabbed the notebook and wrote, "FUMES!"

"Exactly," I said. "The painters told us that Laura wouldn't be coming home tonight. Because of the paint fumes. I mean, would you want to stay in your apartment the night it was painted?"

"The painters could have been wrong about her plans," Jamal said with a shrug. "I don't think that proves much."

"Maybe she has nowhere else to sleep," Casey pointed out.

"Or what if . . . ," I said. And then it was as if all the hair on my head stood straight up. It didn't, but that's what it felt like. "Oh, wow," I said, only I was so scared, barely any sound came out.

"What?" said the whole team at once.

I looked around the pier. Most of the cars were gone—only a few cabs were left, cruising for rides. The place was quickly turning back into a dark, deserted waterfront, which only scared me more. I lowered my voice. "What if that wasn't Laura who got into that cab?"

"What? Why?" said Gaby, her face looking as scared as mine.

I told them about the wisps of blond hair I'd seen sticking out from under the red wig on the young woman in Captain

Blood's cabin. "That woman who just got into that cab was a fake Laura. They were trying to throw us off!"

Hector frowned. Then he shook his head. Smiling, he wrote, "Mystery-itis."

"It's not mystery-itis!" I practically shrieked. "They're trying to kill Laura! I know they are!"

Mr. Nguyen was giving me a look as if maybe I was going to need to spend some time in a hospital. "First of all," he said gently, "I doubt very much that that was a fake Laura, as you say. But let's just say you're right and they're trying to kill this woman. Why? Why would they want to kill her? It doesn't make sense. You know I like to read mysteries myself. They always have to explain the motive.

"Anyway," Mr. Nguyen said, "I have no more time for mysteries. We are going." He hailed two of the last cabs at the pier. He opened one cab door and guided me inside. Hector, Gaby, and Casey followed me in. Mr. Nguyen stuck his head inside the cab, gave directions to the driver and cab fare to us. Then he and the rest of the team headed for the other cab.

"I think that's the maddest I've ever seen him," Gaby said.

"I've seen him madder," Casey said. She was scrunched into the seat right next to me. "The time I put the plastic rolls in his bread basket. He went nuts."

I wasn't listening. I was thinking about something Mr. Nguyen had just said. "I have no more time for mysteries." *Time* . . . that was the word that triggered the explosion in my brain.

"Hector," I said. "What time is it?"

Hector looked at his watch.

He growled in amazement. His watch was gone.

"Hmm . . . Presto must have really stolen it on the subway after all," I said. "But we can't worry about that now."

Casey pulled her arm free from where it was pinned next to me. She peered at her watch in the dark. "It's eleven-sixteen." By the look on Hector's face, I could tell he had just figured out what I was getting at. He made a strangled sound as he tried to yell at the cabdriver to stop. No words came out, but the driver was so startled he screeched to a halt anyway. Hector flung open the door and started running back down the pier.

I ran after him, with Gaby and Casey running alongside me, both yelling at me to tell them what was going on.

"Captain . . . Andersen said he promised . . . to get the ship back by . . . eleven," I explained as I ran. "But on the phone, Ed Poe said . . . she'd be . . ."

I didn't have to finish. Gaby had it now. Gaby's got a mind like a computer. She probably could recite half the messages that Ghostwriter had brought the team that afternoon. Now the message she repeated was:

"Dead at midnight."

21

I glanced back over my shoulder as I ran. At the other end of the pier, the other cab had stopped as well, and the rest of the team was running after us. Mr. Nguyen yelled and waved his arms for them to stop. Then he started running, too.

I was running fast. I was praying we weren't too late. I reached the edge of the pier and skidded to a halt. I almost fell right into the murky water.

The gangplank had been removed. The ship lay anchored about fifty yards away, but there was no way to get to it. That sure seemed fishy. If I had had any doubts left about what was happening, this would have settled it. Most big ships I'd seen always sat right at the dock.

We ran back down the wharf and down to the edge of

the water. I was getting ready to dive in, even though the water looked disgusting. But then—

"Rowboat!" Casey cried, pointing.

There were several rowboats, in fact, tied up about a hundred yards away. We raced along the shore toward them. The boats were black, all marked RAVEN. Someone had taken the trouble to hide these boats out of the way. More proof.

Gaby and Hector undid the rope tying one of the boats to a metal pole by the shore, and we climbed in. Hector and Gaby sat in the middle, each rowing with one oar. Casey sat in the back, writing a message for the rest of the team.

Ghostwriter didn't have to carry the message far. Alex, Jamal, and Tina were already climbing into another rowboat. And Mr. Nguyen wasn't far behind.

Up ahead, like a dark mountain, loomed the *Raven.*

"How do we get in?" Gaby wondered.

I had no idea. In fact, I felt the way I'd felt that afternoon when I was staring at my computer screen. Not only didn't I have an idea, I felt sure I never *would* have an idea.

But all the time I was thinking this, I was staring at the anchor line hanging off the front of the *Raven.* And when I stopped telling myself that I wouldn't get an idea, I realized there was an idea staring me in the face.

"Row toward that anchor line!" I cried.

Climbing up a wet, black cable in the rain and the dark when you're in the middle of a cold, polluted river—it's not the easiest thing in the world. But I was the first one out of the rowboat. I started making my way up the cable, hand over hand.

By the time I was halfway up, I knew I was going to fall. But then I saw the gold letters on the ship's side—THE

RAVEN. Ghostwriter pulled out five letters and spun them, pulsing a gold message: **NERVE!**

Ghostwriter gave me new confidence. I made it to the railing of the lower deck. Up and over. Then I helped Casey up, and Casey and I helped Gaby and Hector. And then we all helped Tina, Alex, and Jamal and—

No one was saying a word. The dark, deserted ship was a scary place—a lot scarier than it had been during the party. But that wasn't why we were all so silent. We could hear someone talking. It was Ed Poe.

We crept around the gangway. There he stood. He had Laura tied up and leaning against the railing. He was talking to her.

"I'm serious, Laura," he said. "If you don't tell me the truth, I'm going to throw you right over the side of the ship. Now you don't want that, I'm sure."

"I can't—swim," she said softly. There was terror in her voice, but she was trying not to show it.

"Exactly," said Ed Poe.

"But I promise you," Laura pleaded, "I didn't tell my idea to anyone! Not a single soul. You scared me so much about someone stealing it, I was afraid to. Why won't you believe me?"

"And you didn't write it down?"

"No, I swear!"

"Good." Another big smile from Ed Poe. "I just wanted to make absolutely, positively, totally, certainly sure. Now my plan will work perfectly."

A stunned silence from Laura. And from me. I was thinking one word. *Motive.*

"Laura, do you think I'm a good writer?" asked Ed Poe.

"Yes, of course, Mr. Poe, I—"

"Well, I'm not. I'm a great writer. Perhaps the greatest mystery writer who ever lived. And what's become of me? I play a lousy pirate in return for free room and board on this gloomy houseboat. For twenty years—*twenty years*—I've been stuck in my search for a new idea for a mystery. And now . . ." He raised a fist to the dark sky. "Now I've got it!"

He smiled at Laura. "My daughter, Beverly, looks a lot like you, wouldn't you say, Laura? Same height, same build. In the dark, with a red wig, from a distance, no one would ever guess. So tonight when Beverly got in that cab and waved goodbye, she provided me with one hundred witnesses who will back up my alibi. They'll all say you went home. And then there are ten dockworkers who can testify that I spent the night on board the ship. So when you disappear, which you're about to do, no one will ever so much as think of accusing me." He cackled. "And besides, what's my motive? So you see, Laura, it's the perfect crime."

And with that he clapped a hand over Laura's mouth so that she couldn't scream. Then he picked her up and started to push her over the railing to her death.

22

We all started running at once, like a cavalry charge. Everyone was shouting. Except Hector, who made that weird garbled scream of his.

Stunned, Ed Poe let go of Laura, who slid to the wet deck beneath his feet. We tried to tackle him. But when we hit him, he flew right over the side of the ship.

So did I.

23

Well, that's the end of my story, pretty much.

I know the last thing I told you was about me falling off the ship. I guess you could say things went downhill from there.

But seriously . . .

It was a very lucky thing Mr. Nguyen had rowed after us. Because he was the one who fished me out of the East River. I was flailing around like crazy and screaming. I almost capsized the rowboat before Mr. Nguyen was able to pull me in.

Ed Poe swam for it, and we let him go. We figured we'd let the police take care of him. And they did.

Right now he's under arrest for attempted murder. I hope they lock him up for life. I mean, not only was he going to steal someone else's idea, he was going to kill for it. I know what it's like, needing an idea for a story. But there's no excuse for what he tried to do. No excuse in the world.

And just think, if I hadn't been stuck on an idea myself, we never would have caught him.

Laura was really grateful to us, of course, for saving her life. She said she didn't have any money to pay us a reward, but she made us all come over to her place the next night for dinner. And when I told her about my writing problems, she offered to be my writing buddy. She said we could call each other whenever we were stuck on a problem in one of our stories.

Thanks to my new writing buddy, the next two weeks flew by, and before I knew it, it was Sunday again. Another beautiful spring afternoon. I was back at my computer, writing my mystery. I forgot to mention that after Ms. Serling heard what had happened to me, she gave me a new deadline. Tomorrow morning, nine sharp.

This time I got started right away. I was going to write about what happened—searching for Laura, Ed Poe, the *Raven,* the whole bit. But then I remembered I'd have to leave out Ghostwriter, and that just didn't seem fair. It would also ruin the story, as far as I was concerned.

So instead, my mystery was about this girl whose mom died when she was seven, and now she had these earrings of her mom's that meant a whole lot to her. And then the earrings were stolen.

Sound familiar? I know, some of my mystery was true, but most of it I made up. Best of all, writing the story was helping me. Because today is Mom's birthday.

Always a hard day for me, like I said. But I'd been putting a lot of my feelings and memories into the story, and it made me feel better. Also, whenever I got stuck, I called Laura.

Laura turned out to be nothing like the person I imagined from the painting. So my first impression was wrong again. On the other hand, I like the real Laura even more.

For instance, Laura is great to talk to about writing problems. It was Laura who suggested I write about Mom. Laura said it helped to choose things you feel really strongly about. And it made the writing better, too.

By the way, Laura is busy writing her mystery novel, using the idea she almost got killed for. She wanted to tell me the idea, but I wouldn't let her. I made her promise not to tell anyone else until it's finished!

Speaking of finishing . . . I stared at my computer screen for a moment, then picked up the phone.

"Done," I told Laura. "All except those last two words."

She clapped. "That's great, Lenni! Way to go. I'm only halfway through my first chapter."

"You'll get there," I said glumly.

"Hey, if you're finished, how come you sound so down?"

"I don't know. You said there's nothing more exciting than when you finish writing something. But I'm kind of sad about it, too. I guess 'cause it means saying goodbye to my characters."

"I've got a solution," Laura said. "Tomorrow night you start a new story."

I smiled. "All right! And then can we, you know, keep being writing buddies?"

"I'm counting on it," Laura said. "After all, I've got twenty more chapters to go."

We talked awhile longer; then she had to get back to work. After we hung up, I stared at the screen. With two fingers, I typed out the last two words:

The End

COMING SOON
FROM GHOSTWRITER

Cow-Eating Fish
And Other Amazing Animals

by Christina Wilsdon

How do animals hide, find food, talk to each other, and get around? You'll find more fun facts than you can shake a snake at or sink your claws into in this terrific trivia book. Do you know:

- why flamingos are pink?
- what a chimp's favorite snack is?
- which animal shoots a six-foot spray of blood at its enemies?

You'll also find an animal mystery in every chapter that can be solved only when you use your human smarts and your animal instincts!